COU
L I

COUNTRY LEGACY

EMMETT

NEW YORK TIMES BESTSELLING AUTHOR

Diana Palmer

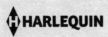

Recycling programs
for this product may
not exist in your area.

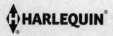

ISBN-13: 978-1-335-52313-6

Emmett
First published in 1992. This edition published in 2022.
Copyright © 1992 by Diana Palmer

This edition published by arrangement with Harlequin Books S.A.

For questions and comments about the quality of this book,
please contact us at CustomerService@Harlequin.com.

Harlequin Enterprises ULC
22 Adelaide St. West, 41st Floor
Toronto, Ontario M5H 4E3, Canada
www.Harlequin.com

Printed in U.S.A.

A prolific author of more than one hundred books, **Diana Palmer** got her start as a newspaper reporter. A *New York Times* bestselling author and voted one of the top ten romance writers in America, she has a gift for telling the most sensual tales with charm and humor. Diana lives with her family in Cornelia, Georgia. Visit her website at dianapalmer.com.

Chapter 1

The office was in chaos. Melody Cartman eyed the window ledge with keen speculation and wondered if standing out there might get her a few minutes' reprieve. She glanced toward her newly married third cousin, Logan Deverell, and his beaming wife, Kit, and decided that she couldn't spoil their honeymoon.

"You'll cope," Kit promised in a whisper. "Just tell everyone he'll be back in touch with them next week and that Tom Walker is handling all his accounts until he returns."

"Has he told Mr. Walker that?" Melody asked, acutely aware of Mr. Walker's temper. Tom had started out in New York City, but circumstances had brought him to Houston. Texas, he'd once said, reminded him a little of his native South Dakota. Melody had often wondered if he'd been brought up by a mountain lion there, because on occasion he could give a pretty good imitation of one.

"Honest." Kit put her hand over her heart. "I swear Logan spoke to him first this time. I heard him with my own ears."

"That's all right then. Honestly he seemed like such a nice man when I first met him. But I took him that client of Mr. Deverell's and found him involved in giving another client the bum's rush out the door. Our client and the other client both ran for it, and I was left to face the music. He never used a bad word or the same word twice, but I was three inches shorter when I escaped from his office."

"Logan is your third cousin. Can't you call him Logan?"

Melody glanced toward the big, dark man on the telephone in his office. "Not without a head start," she said finally.

"Anyway, he didn't volunteer Tom without mentioning it to him this time, so you won't get your ears burned. Think you can handle everything for a week?"

"If I can't cope by now, I'll never be able

to," Melody said, and her brave smile made her look almost pretty. She was a tall woman, very country-looking in some ways, with freckles and a softly rounded face that was framed by long, blond-streaked light brown hair. Her eyes were brown, with tiny flecks of gold in them. If she took the time, she could look very attractive, Kit thought. But Melody wore jumpers with long-sleeved blouses, or tailored suits, and always in colors that were much better suited to the coloring of someone with dark hair and an equally dark complexion.

"You'd like Tom if you got to know him," Kit told her. "He knocked that man out the door for some pretty blatant sexual harassment of his secretary. He's only bad tempered when he needs to be, and he's all alone except for a married sister back home and a nephew. He doesn't even go out with women."

"I can see why...!"

"Not nice," Kit chided. "He's a good-looking, intelligent man, and he's rich."

"I can think of at least one ax murderer with the same description. I read about him in there." She gestured toward one of the supermarket tabloids.

Kit's eyes fell to the tabloid on Melody's desk, its cover carrying color photos of a particularly gruesome murder. "Do you actually read this stuff?" Kit asked with a grimace. "These photos are terrible!"

"I thought you were a detective," Melody said. "Aren't detectives supposed to be used to stuff like that?"

Kit smiled sheepishly. "Well, I don't detect those sort of cases."

"I don't blame you. Actually I didn't buy it for the grisly pictures. I bought it for this nifty reducing diet. Doesn't it look interesting? You don't give up any foods, you simply cut down and cut out sweets."

"You aren't fat, Melody," the other woman pointed out.

"No, I'm just big. I do wish I were slender and willowy," she said wistfully.

"There isn't a thing wrong with the way you are."

"That's what you think! Actually I—"

A sudden commotion in the hall cut her off. She and Kit turned just as Emmett Deverell and his three children walked in. The kids were wearing costumes left over from their Thanksgiving Day play last month—Indian costumes.

Guy, the eldest, stood beside his father and glared at Melody. But Amy and Polk, the younger kids, made a beeline for their favorite person in the office.

"Hi, Kit!" they said in unison. "Hello, Melody. Can we sit and watch TV with you for a while?"

"Please?" Amy ventured, looking up at Melody with eyes that were the same shade of green as her father's. "We'll be ever so good. Emmett has to get our airplane tickets and Polk and I don't want to go to the airport. We got to be in the parade in the rodeo!"

"You all look very nice," Melody told them.

Guy ignored her.

Polk had already turned on the TV and was staring at the screen. "Aw, gee, Big Bird isn't on right now, Amy," he said miserably.

Melody glanced at the kids, noticing again how much they all favored their father. Guy came closest. He was tall, too, with a lean face and dark hair. Amy looked a lot like her mother, Adell, except for those green eyes. All the kids had them.

The last time Emmett had been in the office, he'd savaged Melody. The San Antonio rancher hated her and made no secret of the fact. He didn't approve of her working for Logan, who was a relative of his as well, but by blood, not marriage, as Melody was. Melody had had several days to remember and burn over his attitude. She was through being intimidated by him. He might be almost a generation older than she was, but he wasn't going to walk on her feelings anymore.

"Amy and Polk want to stay with you while I go to the airport," Emmett said icily. He didn't mention leaving Guy, because Guy disliked Melody as much as Emmett did.

Melody cocked an eyebrow, and tried to stay calm. She was melting with fear inside, but she wasn't going to let him know it. "Am I being asked?" she replied formally.

Emmett's pale green eyes glittered at her. "Yes, if you want the whole ten yards."

"In that case, Amy and Polk are welcome to watch TV while you're gone," she said, triumphant with her small victory.

Emmett didn't like the challenge in her dark eyes, or that tiny smirk. If those kids hadn't been giving him hell all morning, he wouldn't even be here. He was surly with bad temper.

"You won't help them run away or anything?" he asked, with a sarcastic, pointed reference to her part in his ex-wife Adell's sudden departure with Melody's brother, Randy.

He wasn't going to do that to her, she promised herself. She wasn't going to let him play on her conscience. Her eyes settled on the tabloid and it triggered a memory; something Kit had elaborated on since her return from Emmett's house in San Antonio. She smiled sweetly and picked up the tabloid. "Have you seen the latest on that ax murder, Mr. Deverell?" she asked, and stuck the gory front page under his arrogant nose.

He turned green instantly. "Damn you…!" He choked before his mad dash to the restroom.

Melody and Polk and Amy and Kit chuckled helplessly. Guy glared at them and walked out to find his father.

"He has a stomach of glass," Melody pronounced, recalling Kit's revelations about how easily Emmett could be made ill with even talk of gory things. Amazing, for a rancher who was also something of a rodeo star. It was one of many paradoxes about Emmett that would have fascinated a less prejudiced woman. She took the paper and stuck it into her purse. She could use it as a talisman against future attack by Emmett. "Make yourselves comfortable, kids," she told Amy and Polk.

"That was a dirty trick." Kit laughed.

"He deserved it. Nasty, arrogant beast," she muttered, glaring at the door into the hall as if he were hiding there waiting to pounce. "If he can't take it, he shouldn't dish it out."

Kit was trying not to laugh too hard. Logan joined them, affectionately slipping an arm around his wife. "If we can't dish what out?"

"Melody made Emmett sick," Amy volunteered. "Look what's on educational television, Melody! It's Reading Rainbow!"

"Good, good," Melody said absently.

"How did you make Emmett sick?" Logan asked curiously.

"Never mind. We women have to have our secret weapons, especially when it comes to people like your cousin Emmett," Kit told him. "Melody, I've given you a number where we can be reached if you need to contact us."

"I'll only use it if there's an emergency," Melody promised.

Kit smiled at her. "I know that."

"And don't let Tom give you fits," Logan told her. "He's not a bad man. It was my fault. I should have told him he was being volunteered to handle my clients that afternoon, but I was in a rush to get married."

"I remember." Melody chuckled. "It's okay. I'll manage."

"If you can't, you might turn those kids loose on him," Logan suggested.

"Don't give her any ideas. We have to leave, right now," Kit said mirthfully, tugging at her husband's arm. "Take care, Melody."

"Yes, and don't let my cousin walk on you," Logan added. "You're my secretary, not his paid babysitter. Keep that in mind."

"I will."

"So long."

They walked out the door just as a pale, subdued Emmett was coming back in with Guy at his heels.

"That wasn't fair," Guy said angrily, glaring at Melody.

"You kids did it to him," she pointed out. "Kit told me all about it."

"We're family. You're not!"

"Yes, she is," Amy argued. "She's our aunt. Isn't that right, Emmett?"

He looked even worse. "I'll be back for Amy and Polk about three o'clock," he said without answering the question.

"But isn't she our aunt?" Amy persisted.

"She's our stepaunt," Polk told her.

"Oh." She was satisfied and went back to watching TV. "Do take care of Emmett, Guy, and don't let him get run over by any buses."

"I don't need taking care of," Emmett muttered. "But she might," he added with a glare at Melody.

"Watch it," Logan advised sotto voce. "She slipped that tabloid into her purse."

"Turncoat!" Kit gasped, hitting her husband's shoulder.

"We men have to stick together," Logan told her, chuckling. "In today's world, there's nothing more endangered than a male. Any day now, the women's lib movement will start passing out hit lists and organizing death squads to wipe out men."

"Wouldn't surprise me." Emmett sighed. "The way it looks, we're evolving into an Amazon society where men will be used to procreate the species and then efficiently be put to death."

Melody eyed Emmett. "What an interesting idea."

"Shame on you!" Kit chuckled. "Honestly, the radicals just get all the publicity. Most women's libbers just want a fair shake—equal pay and equal rights. What's so terrible about that?"

"And there are men who are just as prejudiced against women." Logan drew Kit close. "Haven't you ever heard of the battle of the sexes? It's been around since time began. It's just getting better press."

"I suppose so." Melody sighed. "Maybe men aren't endangered after all."

"Thank you," Emmett said tersely. "I'm glad to know that I won't have to stand guard at my front door to ward off women death squads."

"Oh, I wouldn't go that far," Melody advised.

"Wouldn't you?" Emmett muttered. "And I thought you were a little shrinking violet."

"More like a Venus flytrap, actually," she replied brightly. "I thought you were going to the airport to get tickets home?"

"Notice how much enthusiasm she put into that question?" Logan asked with pure relish. "And you said women wouldn't leave you alone. This must be refreshing for you."

Emmett didn't look refreshed. He looked as if he might explode momentarily. "Let's go, Guy. Have a nice honeymoon, you two," he added to Logan and Kit. "I don't think much of marriage, but good luck anyway."

"Our mama ran off and left him," Amy volunteered. "Emmett doesn't want to marry anybody."

"But he must," Polk said with a serious

frown. "Isn't he always bringing those real glittery, pretty ladies home?"

"Don't be silly," Guy said urbanely. "Those are good-time girls. You don't marry them."

"What's a good-time girl?" Amy asked.

"Just the same as a good-time boy, only shorter," Melody said with icy delight, and she smiled at Emmett.

He went two shades darker.

"Time to go," Kit said quickly. "Emmett, can we give you a lift? We're going straight to the airport."

"Yes," Logan said, taking his tall cousin's muscular arm in a big hand. "Come along, Guy. See you in a week, Melody. If you have any problems, call me. And if you could check on Tansy in the hospital, I'd appreciate it. Chris is watching out for her, but you can't have too many observers where my mother is concerned."

"Certainly I will," Melody agreed. "I don't have much to do in the evenings, anyway."

"I didn't think there would be a man that brave," Emmett agreed.

Melody reached for her purse. Emmett spared her a glance that promised retribution before he made a quick exit with the others.

* * *

The chaos began to calm with Logan's exit. The telephones rang for an hour or two. After that, there were only a few calls and two clients who came in person to ask about their investments. Melody had the figures. It was only a matter of pulling them up—her boss had given her permission before he left—and showing them to the visitors.

The kids were amazingly good. They watched educational programming without a peep, except to ask for change for the soft drink machine. Melody gave it to them and then listened worriedly for sounds of the machine being mugged. Fortunately there was no such noise, and she settled down to the first peace she'd had all day.

She managed to clear her desk of work before Emmett showed up, late, to pick up the kids.

"Aw, do we have to go?" Polk groaned. "Mr. Rogers is coming on!"

"Yes, we have to go. We're leaving for home in the morning, thank God. Only one more event to go tonight—bareback bronc riding."

"Isn't that one of the most dangerous events?" Melody asked.

His eyebrows arched under the wide-brimmed Stetson he hadn't bothered to remove from his dark hair. "Any rodeo event is dangerous if a contestant is stupid or careless. I'm neither."

She knew that already. He was something of a legend in rodeo. He wouldn't be aware that she'd followed his career. She was a rodeo fan, but Emmett's attitude toward her had kept her silent about her interest in the sport.

"Thank you for letting us stay with you, Melody," Amy said, smiling up at her.

Melody smiled back. She liked the little girl very much. She was open and warm and loving, despite her mischievous nature.

Emmett saw that smile and felt it all the way to his toes. He couldn't have imagined even a minute before that a smile could change a plain face and make it radiate beauty. But he saw the reality of it in Melody's soft features. Involuntarily his eyes fell to her body. She was what a kind man would call voluptuous, her form and shape perfectly proportioned but just a tad past slender. Adell had been bacon-thin. Melody was her exact opposite.

It irritated him that he should notice Melody in that way. She was nothing to him except a turncoat. She and her brother had disrupted and destroyed his life. Not only his, but his children's, as well. He could easily have hated her for that.

"I said, let's go," he told the children.

"Okay." Polk sighed.

"I'll wait in the hall," Guy murmured. He avoided even looking at Melody.

"Guy hates you," Amy told her with blunt honesty. "But I think you're wonderful."

"I think you're wonderful, too," Melody replied.

Amy grinned and walked up to her father. "We can go now, Emmett. Can I write to my friend Melody?"

"We'll talk about it," Emmett said noncommittally. "Thanks for watching them," he said as an afterthought.

"Oh, it was my plea…sure!" She tripped over a tomahawk that someone had left lying on the floor and ended up on her back. Guy picked up the weapon, and the kids and Emmett made a circle around her prone body. She glared up at them, trying not to think how a sacrificial victim in an Indian encampment might have felt. In those Indian costumes, the kids looked eerie.

"Whose tomahawk?" Emmett asked as he reached down and pulled Melody up with a minimum of strain. His hand made hers tingle. She wondered if he'd felt the excitement of the contact, too, because he certainly let go of her fast.

"It's mine, Emmett," Amy said, sighing. She looked up at him, pushing back her pigtails, and her green eyes were resigned. "Go ahead and hit me. I didn't mean to make Melody hurt herself, though. I like her."

"I know you didn't mean it," Melody said, and smiled. "It's okay, nothing dented."

"Next time, be more careful where you put that thing," Emmett muttered.

"That's right, Amy," Melody said, nodding. "Between your father's ears would be a good place."

He glared at her. "You didn't hear that, Amy. Let's go, kids."

He herded the children out the door and closed it. Melody sat by herself with no ringing phones, no blaring television, no laughing children. Her life and the office were suddenly empty.

She closed up precisely at 5:00 p.m. and went by the grocery store to get enough for the weekend, which was just beginning. Thanksgiving Day had been quiet and lonely. She'd had a turkey breast, but she and Alistair had finished it off for supper the night before. So she bought ground beef for hamburgers and a small beef roast and vegetables to make stew and, later, soup. She lived on a budget, which meant that she bypassed steak and frozen éclairs. She would have loved to indulge her taste for both. Maybe someday, she thought wistfully…

She fed Alistair, her big marmalade tabby, and then made herself a light supper. She ate it with little enthusiasm. Then she curled up with Alistair on the sofa to watch a movie on television. During the last scene, a very interesting standoff between a murderer and the police, the telephone started ringing. She grimaced, hating the interruption. If she answered it, she'd surely miss the end of the movie she'd been watching for two hours. She ignored it at first. The only people who ever telephoned her were people who were selling things. But whoever was calling wouldn't give up. It stopped, briefly, only to start ringing insistently again. This time she was afraid not to answer it. It might be Kit or Logan or Tansy or even her brother.

She picked up the receiver. "Hello?"

"Is this Miss Melody Cartman?" a crisp, professional voice asked.

"Yes."

"I'm Nurse Willoughby. We have a Mr. Emmett Deverell here at city general hospital with a massive concussion. He's only just regained consciousness. He gave us your name and asked us to call and have you pick up his children at the Mellenger Hotel."

Melody stood frozen in place. The only thing that registered was that Emmett was hurt and she'd become a babysitter. She could hardly say no or argue. Concussions were terribly dangerous.

"The children are…where?"

"At the Mellenger Hotel. Room three hundred and something. He's very foggy at the moment and in a great deal of pain."

"He will be all right?" Melody asked, hating herself for being concerned.

"We hope so," came the crisp reply.

"Tell him that I'll look after the children," she said.

"Very well."

The phone went dead before she could ask another question. She stared around her like someone in a trance. Where in the world was she going to put three renegade children, one of whom hated her? And how long was she going to have them?

For one insane moment, she thought about calling Adell and Randy, but she dismissed that idea at once. Emmett would never forgive her. At the moment, he deserved a little consideration, she supposed.

She got her coat and took a cab to the hotel. It was very late to be driving around Houston, and her little car was unreliable in wet weather. Houston was notorious for flooding, and the rain was coming down steadily now.

She asked at the desk for Emmett's room number, quickly explaining the circumstances to a sympathetic desk clerk after giving Emmett's condition and the hospital's number, so that management could check her story if they felt the need to. In fact, they did, and she didn't blame them. These days, one simply couldn't turn over three children to a total stranger who might or might not intend them harm.

When she got to the hotel room, there were muffled sounds from within. Melody, who knew the kids all too well, knocked briefly but firmly on the door.

There was a sudden silence, followed by a scuffle and a wail. The door flew open and a matronly lady with frazzled hair almost fell on Melody with relief.

"Are you their mother?" the elderly woman asked. "I'm Mrs. Johnson. Here they are, safe and sound, my fee will be added to the hotel bill. You are their mother?"

"Well, no," she began.

"Oh, my God!"

"I'm to take charge of them," Melody added, because it looked as if the woman might be preparing to have a heart attack on the spot.

A wavery smile replaced the horror on the woman's lined face. "Then I'll just be off. Good night!"

"Chicken," Amy muttered, peering around Melody to watch the woman's incredibly fast retreat.

"What have you three been up to?" Melody asked, glaring at them.

"Nothing at all, Melody, dear," Amy said sweetly, and grinned.

"She just wasn't used to kids, I guess," Polk added. He grinned, too.

Behind them there were the remains of two foam-filled pillows and what appeared to be the ropes that closed the heavy curtains.

"We had a pillow fight," Amy explained.

"And then we went skiing in the bathroom," Polk said.

Melody could barely see the bathroom. The door was ajar and the floor seemed to be soaked. She was beginning to understand her predecessor's agile retreat. Days and days... of this. She wouldn't have an apartment left! And all because she felt sorry for a man who had to be her worst enemy.

"Why are you here?" Guy asked belligerently. "Where's Dad?"

That brought her back to her original purpose for being there. Emmett's accident.

She sat down on the sofa, tossing her purse beside her, while she struggled to find the right words to tell them.

"Something's happened," Guy said when he saw her face. He stiffened. "What?"

Even at such a young age, he was already showing signs of great inner strength, of ability to cope with whatever life threw at him. Amy and Polk looked suddenly vulnerable, but not Guy.

"Your father has a brain concussion," Melody told them. "He's conscious now, but in a lot of pain. He'll have to stay in the hospital for a day or so. Meanwhile, he wants you to come home with me."

"He hates you," Guy said coldly. "Why would he want us to stay with you?"

"Because I'm all you've got," Melody replied. "Unless you'd rather I called the juvenile authorities…?"

Guy's massive self-confidence failed. He shrugged and turned away.

Amy climbed onto Melody's lap and clung. "Our daddy will be all right, won't he?" she asked tearfully.

"Of course he will," Melody assured her, gathering her close. "He's very tough. It will take more than a concussion to keep him down."

"Yes, it will," Polk said. He turned away because his lower lip was trembling.

"Let's get your things together and go," Melody said. "Have you had something to eat?"

"We had pizza and chocolate sundaes."

Melody could imagine that the elderly lady in charge of them had agreed with any menu that would keep them quiet. But she'd have to get some decent food into them. That would give her something to work toward. Meanwhile, she found herself actually worrying about Emmett. The first thing she was going to do when they got to the apartment was phone the hospital and get an update. Surely Emmett was indestructible, wasn't he?

She looked at the children and felt a surge of pity for them. She knew how it felt to be alone. When their parents had died, Randy had worked at two jobs to support them, while Melody was still in school. She'd carried her share of the load, but it had been lonely for both of them. She hoped these children wouldn't have the same ordeal to face that she and Randy had.

Chapter 2

The nurse on duty in Emmett's ward told Melody that Emmett would have to be confined for at least two days. He was barely conscious, but they were cautiously optimistic about his condition.

Melody was assured that she and the children would be allowed to see him the next day, during visiting hours. In the meantime, she scoured her apartment to find enough blankets and pillows for three sleepy children. She put two of them in her bed, and one of them on a cot that had belonged to Randy when he was a boy. She slept on her own pullout sofa bed, and was delighted to find that it wasn't terribly uncomfortable.

It was fortunate that she had the weekend to look after the children. Having to juggle them, along with her job, would have been a real headache. She'd have coped. But how?

They had a change of clothing. Getting them to change, though, was the trick.

"This isn't dirty—" Guy indicated a shirt limp and dingy and smelly from long wear "—and I won't change it."

"I'm all right, too," Polk said, grinning at her.

"We're fine, Melody," Amy agreed. She patted the woman's hand in a most patronizing way. "Now, you just get dressed yourself and don't worry about us, all right?"

Melody counted to ten. "We're going to see your father," she said calmly. "Don't you want him to think you look nice?"

"Oh, Emmett never notices unless we go naked, Melody," Amy assured her.

"And sometimes not even then," Polk said with a chuckle. "Dad's very absentminded when he's rodeoing."

"He sure doesn't seem to notice what the three of you get up to," she said quietly.

"We like our dad just the way he is," Guy

said belligerently. "Nobody bad-mouths our dad."

"I wasn't bad-mouthing him," Melody said through her teeth. "Can we just go to the hospital now?"

"Sure," Guy said, folding his thin arms over his chest. "But I'm not changing clothes."

She threw up her hands. "Oh, all right," she muttered. "Have it your way. But if your clothes set off the sprinkler system, I'm climbing into a broom closet so nobody will know who brought you."

At the hospital, Melody herded them off the elevator and down the hall to the nurses' station.

"Look at all the gadgets." Polk whistled, peering over the counter at the computers. "Wouldn't I love to play with that!"

"Bite your tongue," Melody said under her breath. She smiled at an approaching nurse. "I'm Melody Cartman. You have an Emmett Deverell on this floor with a concussion…?"

A loud roar, followed by, "You're not putting that damned thing under me!" caught their attention.

"Indeed we do," the nurse told Melody. "Are

you a concerned relative anxious to transfer him to another hospital?" she added hopefully.

"I'm afraid not," Melody said. "These are his children and they want to see him very much."

"Do you have him tied up in one of those white things?" Amy asked.

"No," the nurse said with a wistful sigh. She turned. "Come on, I'll take you down to his room. Perhaps a diversion will improve his mood."

"I really wouldn't count on it," Melody replied.

"I was afraid you were going to say that. Here we are."

"Dad!" Guy exclaimed, running to his father as a practical nurse laid down a trail of fire getting out the door. "How are you?"

Emmett stared at his eldest blankly. His pale green eyes were bloodshot. His dark hair was disheveled. There was a huge bump on his forehead with stitches and red antiseptic lacing it. He was wearing a white patterned hospital gown and looking as if he'd like to eat half the staff raw.

"It's almost noon," he informed Melody. "Where in hell have you been? Get me out of here!"

"Don't worry, Dad, we'll spring you," Guy promised, with a wary glance toward the nurse.

"You can't leave today, Mr. Deverell," the young nurse said apologetically. "Dr. Miller said that you must stay for at least forty-eight hours. You've had a very severe concussion. You can't go walking around the streets like that. It's very dangerous."

Emmett glared at her. "I hate it here!"

The nurse looked as if she might bite through her tongue trying not to reply in kind. She forced a smile. "I'm sure you do. But you can't leave yet. I'll leave you to visit with your family. I'm sure you're glad to see your wife and children."

"She's not the hell my wife!" Emmett raged. "I'd rather marry a pit viper!"

"I assure you that the feeling is mutual," Melody said to the nurse.

The woman leaned close on her way out the door. "Dr. Miller escaped. When he comes back, I'll beg on my knees for sedation for Mr. Deverell. I swear."

"God bless you," Melody said fervently.

"What are you mumbling about?" Emmett demanded when the nurse left. "And why haven't these kids changed clothes? They smell of pizza and dirt!"

"They wouldn't change," she said defensively.

"You're bigger than they are," he pointed out. "Make them."

She glanced at the kids and shook her head. "Not me, mister. I know when I'm outnumbered. I'm not going to end my days tied to a post imitating barbecue."

"They don't burn people at the stake," he said with exaggerated patience. "That was just gossip about that lady motorist they kidnapped."

"That's right," Polk said. "Gossip."

"Anyway, she got loose before she was very singed." Amy sighed.

Melody gave Emmett a speaking look. It was totally wasted.

"Are you really okay?" Guy asked his father. He, of the three children, was the most worried. He was the oldest. He understood better than they did how serious his father's injury could have been.

"I'm okay," Emmett said. His voice was different when he spoke to the children; it was softer, more tender. He smiled at Guy, and Melody couldn't remember ever being on the receiving end of such a smile. "How about you kids?"

"We're fine," Amy told him. "Melody has a very nice apartment, Emmett. We like it there."

"She has a cat," Polk added. "He's a big orange tabby named Alistair."

"Alistair?" Emmett mused.

"He was a very ordinary-looking cat," Melody said defensively. "The least he deserved was a nice name."

He leaned back against his pillows and closed his eyes. "Saints deliver us."

"I don't think the saints like you very much, Mr. Deverell, on present evidence," she couldn't resist saying.

One bloodshot pale green eye opened. "The saints didn't do this to me. It was a horse. A very nasty-tempered horse whose only purpose in life is to maim poor stupid cowboys who are dim enough to get on him. I let myself get distracted and I came off like a loose hat."

She smiled gently at the description. "I'm sure the horse is crying his eyes out with guilt."

The smile changed her. He liked what he saw. She was vulnerable when her eyes twinkled like that. He opened the other eye, too, and for one long moment they just looked at each other. Melody felt warning bells go off in her head.

"When can you come home, Emmett?" Amy asked, her big eyes on her father.

He blinked and looked down at her. "Two days they said," he replied. "God, I'm sorry about this!" He glanced toward Melody. "I had no right to involve you in my problems."

That sounded like a wholesale apology. Perhaps the head injury had erased his memory so that he'd forgotten her part in Adell's escape.

"I don't mind watching the children for you," she said hesitantly. She pushed back her hair with a nervous hand. "They're no trouble."

"Of course not, they were asleep all night," he replied. "Don't let them out of your sight."

"Aw, Dad," Polk grumbled. "We'll be good."

"Sure we will," Guy said. He glanced at Melody irritably. "If we have to."

"It's only for a day or two," Emmett said. He was feeling foggier by the minute. "I'll reimburse you, of course," he told Melody. He touched his head with an unsteady hand. "God, my head hurts!"

"I guess it does," Melody said gently. She moved closer to the bed, concerned. "Shall I call the nurse?"

"They won't give me anything until the doctor authorizes it, and he's in hiding," he said.

His eyes closed. "Can't say I blame him. I was pretty unhappy about being here."

"I noticed."

He managed a weak chuckle. "If Logan had been at home, you wouldn't be landed with those kids…"

He was asleep.

"Is he going to be okay?" Amy asked. She was chewing her lower lip, looking very young and worried.

Melody smoothed back her hair. "Yes, he'll be fine," she assured the girl. "Come on. We'll go home and I'll make lunch for all of you."

"I want a hot dog," Polk said. "So does Amy."

"I hate hot dogs," Guy replied. "I don't want to stay with you. I'll stay here with Dad."

"You aren't allowed to," Melody pointed out.

He took an angry breath.

"I don't like it any more than you do," she murmured. "But we're stuck with each other. We'd better go."

They followed her out, reluctantly. She stopped long enough to assure the nurse at the desk that she'd bring the kids back the next day to visit their father. She was concerned enough to ask if it was natural for Emmett to go to sleep, and was told that the doctor would check to make sure he was all right.

Guy's dislike of Melody extended to her apartment, her cat, her furniture and especially her cooking.

"I won't eat that," he said forcefully when she put hot dogs and buns and condiments on the table. "I'll starve first."

She knew that it would give him the upper hand if she stooped to arguing with him, so she didn't. "Suit yourself. But we'll have ice cream for dessert and you won't. It's a house rule that you don't get dessert if you don't eat the main course."

"I hate ice cream," he said triumphantly.

"No, he doesn't," Amy said sadly. "He just doesn't like you. He thinks you took our mom away. She won't even write to us or talk to us on the telephone."

"That's right," Guy said angrily. "It's all because of you! Because of your stupid brother!"

He got up, knocking over his chair, and stomped off into the bathroom, slamming the door behind him.

Melody took a bite of her own hot dog, but it tasted like so much cardboard. It was going to be a long two days.

* * *

She didn't know how true her prediction was going to be. Guy sulked for the rest of the day, while she and the other two children watched television and played Monopoly on the kitchen table. While they were going past Go for the tenth time, Guy opened the apartment door and deliberately let Alistair out...

Melody didn't discover that her cat was missing until she started to put his food into his dish.

She looked around, frowning. "Alistair?" she called. The big cat was nowhere in sight. He couldn't have gone out the window. The apartment was on the fourth story and there was no balcony. She searched the apartment, including under the bed, but she couldn't find him.

"Have any of you seen my cat?" she asked.

"Not me," Amy murmured. She was watching cartoons with Polk.

"Me, neither," he said absently.

Guy was staring out the window. He jerked his head, which she assumed meant he hadn't seen the cat.

But he looked odd. She frowned. Alistair had been curled up on the couch just before

Guy had stormed off into the bathroom. She hadn't seen the cat since. But surely the boy wouldn't have done something so heartless as to let the cat out. Surely he wouldn't!

Melody had found Alistair in an alley on her way home from work late one rainy afternoon last year. He'd had a string tied around his neck and was choking. She'd freed him and taken him home. He was flea-infested and pitifully thin, but a trip to the veterinarian and some healthful food had transformed him. He'd been Melody's friend and companion and confidant ever since.

Tears stung her eyes as she searched again, her voice sounding frantic as she called her pet's name with increasing urgency.

Amy got up from the carpet and followed her, frowning. "Can't you find your cat?"

"No," Melody said, her voice raspy. She brushed at a tear on her face.

"Oh, Melody, don't cry!" Amy said. She hugged her. "It will be all right! We'll find him! Polk, Guy," she called sharply. "Come on. Help us hunt for Melody's cat! She can't find him anywhere!"

"Sure," Polk said. "We'll help."

They scoured the apartment. Guy looked,

too, but his cheeks were flushed and he wouldn't meet Melody's eyes.

In desperation, Melody went to the two apartments nearby to ask her neighbors if they'd seen her cat, but no one had noticed him. There was an elevator and a staircase, but there was a door that led to the stairwell and surely it would be closed...

All the same, she checked, and was disturbed to find that the stairwell door was propped open while workmen carried materials to an apartment down the hall that was being renovated.

Leaving the children in the apartment, she rushed down the steps looking for Alistair. She called and called, but there was no answer, and he was nowhere to be found.

Defeated, Melody went back to the apartment. Her expression was so morose that the children knew without asking that she hadn't found the cat.

"I'm sorry," Amy said. "I guess you love him a lot, huh?"

"He's all I have," Melody said without looking up. The pain in her voice was almost tangible. "All I...had."

Guy turned up the television and sat down very close to the screen. He didn't say a word.

Melody cried herself to sleep that night. Randy had Adell, but Melody had no other family. Alistair was the only real family she had left. She was so sick at heart that she didn't know how she was going to stand it. Dismal images of Alistair being run over or chased by dogs and children made her miserable.

She got up early and fixed bacon and eggs before she called the children. They were unnaturally quiet, too, and ate very little. Melody was preoccupied all through the meal. When it was over, she went outside to search some more. But Alistair was nowhere to be found.

Later, she took the kids to the hospital to see Emmett. He was sitting up in a chair looking impatient.

"Get me the hell out of here," he said immediately. "I'm leaving whether they like it or not!"

He seemed to mean it. He was fully dressed, in the jeans and shirt and boots he'd been wearing when they'd taken him to the hospital. The shirt was bloodstained but wearable. He looked pale, even if he sounded in charge of himself.

"What did the doctor say?"

"He said I could go if I insisted, and I'm insisting," Emmett said. "I'll take the kids and go back to the hotel."

Melody went closer to him, clutching her purse. "Mr. Deverell, don't you realize what a risk you'd be taking? If you won't think of yourself, do think of the kids. What will they do if anything happens to you?"

"I won't stay here!" he muttered. "They keep trying to bathe me!"

She managed a faint smile even through her misery. "It's for your own good."

"I'm leaving," he said, his flinty pale green eyes glaring straight into her dark ones.

She sighed. "Well, you can come back with us for today," she said firmly. "I can't let you stagger around Houston alone. My boss would never forgive me."

"Think so?" He narrowed one eye. "I don't need help."

"Yes, you do. One more night won't kill me, I suppose," she added.

"Her cat ran away," Amy said. "She's very sad."

Emmett scowled. "Alistair? How could he run away? Don't you live in an apartment building?"

"Yes. I… He must have gotten out the door," she said, staring down at her feet. "The stairwell door was open, where the workmen were going in and out of the building."

"I'm sorry," he said shortly. He glanced at the kids. Amy and Polk seemed very sympathetic, but Guy was surlier than ever and his lower lip was prominent. Emmett's eyes narrowed.

"Have you checked yourself out?" Melody asked, changing the subject to keep from bursting into tears.

"Yes." He got to his feet, a little unsteadily.

"I'll help you, Dad," Guy said. He propped up his father's side. He wouldn't look at Melody.

"Did you drive or take a cab?" he asked her.

"I drove."

"What do you drive?"

"A Volkswagen," she told him.

He groaned. She smiled for the first time that day. As tall as he was, fitting him inside her small car, even in the front seat, was going to be an interesting experience.

And it was. He had to bring his knees up almost to his chin. Polk and Amy laughed at the picture he made.

"Poor Emmett," Amy said. "You don't fit very well."

"First you shove gory pictures under my nose. Then you stuff me into a tin can with wheels," Emmett began with a meaningful glance in Melody's direction.

"Don't insult my beautiful little car. It isn't the car's fault that you're too tall," she reminded him as she started her car. "And you were horrible to me. I was only getting even."

"I am not too tall."

"I hope you aren't going to collapse," she said worriedly when he leaned his head back against the seat. "I live on the fourth floor."

"I'm all right. I'm just groggy."

"I hope so," she murmured. She put the car in gear and reversed it.

Guy helped him into the elevator and upstairs. Amy and Polk got on the other side, and between them, they maneuvered him into Melody's apartment and onto her sofa.

The sleeping arrangements were going to be interesting, she thought. She could put Emmett and the boys in her bedroom and she and Amy could share the sleeper sofa. It wasn't ideal, but it would be adequate. What wouldn't was managing some pajamas for Emmett.

"I don't wear pajamas," he muttered. "You aren't going to be in the bedroom, so it won't concern you," he added with a glittery green stare.

She turned away to keep him from seeing the color in her cheeks. "All right. I'll see about getting something together for sandwiches."

At least, he wasn't picky about what he ate. That was a mixed blessing. Perhaps it was the concussion, making him so agreeable.

"This isn't bad," he murmured when he'd finished off two egg salad sandwiches.

"Thank you," she replied.

"I hate eggs," Guy remarked, but he was still eating his sandwich as he said it. He didn't look at Melody.

"And me," Melody added for him. He looked up, surprised, and her steady gaze told him that she knew exactly how her cat had managed to get out the door and lost.

He flushed and put down the rest of his sandwich. "I'm not hungry." He got up and went into the living room with Amy and Polk, who were eating on TV tables.

Emmett ran a big hand through his dark hair. "I'm sorry about your cat," he said.

"So am I." She got up and cleared away the dishes. "There's coffee if you'd like some."

"I would. Black."

"I'll bet you don't eat catsup on steak, either," she murmured.

He smiled at her as she put a mug of steaming coffee beside his hand. "Smart girl."

"Why do you ride in rodeos?" she asked when she was sitting down.

The question surprised him. He leaned back in his chair fingering the hot mug, and considered it. "I always have," he began.

"It must be hard on the children, having you away from home so much," she continued. "Even if your housekeeper does look after them."

"They're resourceful," he said noncommittally.

"They're ruined," she returned. "And you know it. Especially Guy."

His eyes narrowed as they met hers. "They're my kids," he said quietly. "And how I raise them is none of your business."

"They're my nephews and niece," she pointed out.

His face went taut under its dark tan. "Don't bring that up."

"Why do you have to keep hiding from it?" she asked miserably. "Randy's my brother. I love him. But he couldn't have taken Adell if she hadn't wanted to go with him…!"

"My God, don't you think I know that?" he asked with bridled fury.

She saw the pain in his face, in his eyes, and

she understood. "But, it wasn't because something was lacking in you," she said softly, trying to make him understand. "It was because she found something in Randy that she needed. Don't you see, it wasn't your fault!"

His whole body clenched. He grimaced and lifted the cup, burning his lips as he forced coffee between them. "It's none of your business," he said gruffly. "Let it alone."

She wanted to pursue the subject, but it wouldn't be wise. She let it go.

"There's a little ice cream," she told him.

He shook his head. "I don't like sweets."

Just like Guy, but she didn't say it. Guy hated her. He hated her enough to let her cat out the door and into the street. Her eyes closed on a wave of pain. It was just as well she wasn't mooning over Emmett, because she was certain that Guy wouldn't let that situation develop.

"You should be in bed," she told Emmett after a tense minute.

"Yes," he agreed without heat and then stood up slowly. "Tomorrow I'll take the kids back to the hotel, and we'll get a flight out to San Antonio. We'll all be out of your hair."

She didn't argue. There was nothing to say.

Chapter 3

Earlier in the day, Melody had telephoned the nearest veterinarian's office and animal shelter, hoping that Alistair might turn up there. But the veterinarian's receptionist hadn't heard of any lost cats, and there was only a new part-time girl at the animal shelter who wasn't very knowledgeable about recent acquisitions. In fact, she'd confided, they'd had a fire the week before, and everything was mixed up. The lady who usually ran the shelter was in the hospital, having suffered smoke inhalation trying to get the animals out. She was very sorry, but she didn't know which cats were new acquisitions and which were old ones.

Melody was sorry about the fire, but she was even more worried about her cat. She went out into the hall one last time to call Alistair, in vain because he didn't appear. She just had to accept that he was gone. It wasn't easy. It was going to be similar to losing a member of her family, and part of her blamed Guy for that. He might hate her, but why had he taken out that hatred on her cat? Alistair had done nothing to hurt him.

Melody slept fitfully, and not only because she was worried about Alistair. The couch was comfortable, as a rule, but Amy was a restless sleeper and it was hard to dodge little flailing arms and legs and not wake up.

Just before daylight, she gave up. She covered the sleeping child, her eyes tender on the little oval face with its light brown hair and straight nose so reminiscent of Adell. Amy's eyes, though, were her father's. All the kids had green eyes, every single one. Adell's were blue, and her hair was light brown. Amy was the one who most resembled her mother, despite her tomboy ways and the temper that matched her father's. That physical resemblance to her mother must have been very painful to Emmett when Adell first left him. Guy seemed to be his favorite, and it wasn't surprising. Guy looked and acted the most like him. Polk was just himself, bespectacled and slight, with no real distinguishing feature except his brain. He seemed to be far and away the brains of the bunch.

She pulled on her quilted robe, her long hair disheveled from sleep, and went slowly into the bathroom, yawning as she opened the door.

Emmett's dark eyebrows levered up when she stopped dead and turned scarlet.

"Sorry!" she gasped, jerking the door back shut.

She went into the living room and sat down in a chair, very quickly. It was disconcerting to find a naked man stepping out of her shower, even if he did have a body that would grace a centerfold in any women's magazine.

He came out a minute later with a towel wrapped around his lean hips. He had an athlete's body, wide shouldered and narrow hipped, and his legs were incredible, Melody thought. She stared at him pie-eyed, trying to act sophisticated when she was just short of starstruck.

"I'm sorry," he said. "I didn't think to lock the door. I assumed this was a little early for you to be up, and I needed a shower."

"Of course."

He frowned as he stared down at her. She was doing her best not to look at him, and her cheeks were flaming. He was an experienced man, and he'd been married. He understood without words why she was reacting so violently to what she'd seen.

"It's all right," he said gently, and he smiled at her. "There's nothing to be embarrassed about."

She swallowed. "Right. Would you like some breakfast?"

"Anything will suit me. I'll get dressed."

She nodded, but she didn't look as he strode back into the bedroom and gently closed the door.

She got up and went to the kitchen, surprised to find that her hands shook when she got the pans out and began to put bacon into one.

Emmett came back while she was breaking eggs into a bowl. He was wearing jeans and a white T-shirt, which stretched over his powerful muscles. He wasn't wearing shoes. He looked rakish and appealing. She pretended not to notice; her memory was giving her enough trouble.

Melody wasn't dressed because she'd forgotten to get her clothes out of the bedroom the night before. That had been an unfortunate oversight, because he was staring quite openly at her in the long green gown and matching quilted robe that fit much too well and showed an alarming amount of bare skin in the deep V neckline. She wasn't wearing makeup, but her blond-streaked brown hair and freckled pale skin gave her enough color to make her interesting to a man.

Emmett realized that she must not know that, because she kept fiddling with her hair after she'd set the eggs aside and started to heat a pan to cook them in.

"Where are the plates?" he asked. He didn't want to add to her discomfort by staring.

"They're up in the cabinet, there—" she gestured "—and so are the cups and saucers. But you don't have to…"

"I'm domesticated," he said gently. "I always was, even before I married." The words, once spoken, dispelled his good mood. He went about setting the table and didn't speak again until he was finished.

Melody had scrambled eggs and taken up the bacon while the biscuits were baking. She took them out of the oven, surprised to see that they weren't overcooked. People in the kitchen made her nervous—Emmett, especially.

"You couldn't get to your clothes, could

you?" he mused. "I should have reminded you last night."

It was an intimate conversation. Having a man in her apartment at all was intimate, and after having met him in the altogether in the bathroom, Melody was more nervous than ever.

"That's all right, I'll dress when the boys get up. You could call them…?"

"Not yet," he replied. "I want to talk to you."

"About what?"

He motioned her into a chair and then sat down across from her, his big, lean hands dangling between his knees as he studied her. "About what you said last night. I've been thinking about it. Did Adell tell you that it was loving Randy, not hating me, that broke up our marriage?"

Melody clasped her hands in her lap and stared at them. "She said that she married you because you were kind and gentle and obviously cared about her so much," she told him, because only honesty would do. "When she met Randy, at the service station where she had her car worked on and bought gas, she tried to pretend it wasn't happening, that she wasn't falling in love. But she was too weak to stop it. I'm not excusing what she did, Emmett," she said when he looked haunted. "There should have been a kinder way. And I should have said no when Randy asked me to help them get away. But nothing will change what happened. She really does love him. There's no way to get around that."

"I see."

He looked grim. She hated the wounded expression on his lean face.

"Emmett," she said gently, "you have to believe it wasn't because of you personally. She fell in love, really in love. The biggest mistake she made was marrying you when she didn't love you properly."

"Do you know what that is?" he asked with a bitter smile. "Loving 'properly'?"

"Well, not really," she said. "I haven't ever been in love." That was true enough. She'd had crushes on movie stars, and once she'd had a crush on a boy back in San Antonio. But that had been a very lukewarm relationship and the boy had gone crazy over a cheerleader who was more willing in the backseat of his car than Melody had been.

"Why?" he asked curiously.

She sighed. "You must have noticed that I'm oversized and not very attractive," she said with a wistful smile.

He frowned. "Aren't you? Who says?"

Color came and went in her cheeks. "Well, no one, but I..."

It disturbed him that he'd said such a thing to her, when she'd been the enemy since Randy had spirited Adell away. "Have the kids given you any trouble?"

"Just Guy," she replied after a minute. "He doesn't like me."

"He doesn't like anybody except me," he said easily. "He's the most insecure of the three."

She nodded. "Amy and Polk are very sweet."

"Adell spoiled them. She favored Guy, although he took it the best of the three when she left. I think he loved her, but he never talks about her."

"He's a very private person, isn't he? Divorce must be hard on everyone," she replied. "My parents loved each other for thirty years—until they died. There was never any question of them getting a divorce or separating. They were happy. So were we. It was a blow when we lost them. Randy wound up being part brother and part parent to me. I was still in school."

"That explains why you were so close, I suppose." He cocked his head and studied her. "How did they die?"

"In a freak accident," she said sadly. "My mother was in very bad health—a semi-invalid. She had what Dad thought was a light heart attack. He got her into the car and was speeding, trying to get her to the hospital. He lost control in a curve and wrecked the car. They both died." She averted her eyes. "There was an oil slick on the road that he didn't see, and a light rain…just enough to bring the oil to the surface. Randy and I blamed ourselves for not insisting that Dad call an ambulance instead of trying to drive her to the emergency room himself. To this day I hate rain."

"I'm sorry," he said kindly. "I lost my parents several years apart, but it was pretty rough just the same. Especially my mother." He was silent for a moment. "She killed herself. Dad had only been dead six months when she was diagnosed with leukemia. She refused treatment, went home and took a handful of barbiturates that they'd given her for pain. I was in my last few weeks of college before graduation. I hadn't started until I was nineteen, so I was late getting out. It was pretty rough, passing my finals after the funeral," he added with a rough laugh.

"I can only imagine," she said sympatheti-
cally.

"I'd already been running the ranch and
going to school as a commuting student. That's
where I met Adell, at college. She was sympathetic and I was so torn up inside. I just wanted
to get married and have kids and not be alone
anymore." He shrugged. "I thought marriage
would ease the pain. It didn't. Nobody cares
like your parents do. When they die, you're
alone. Except, maybe, if you've got kids," he
added thoughtfully, and realized that he hadn't
really paid enough attention to his own kids.
He frowned. He'd avoided them since Adell
left. Rodeo and ranch work had pretty much
replaced parenting with him. He wondered
why he hadn't noticed it until he got hit in the
head.

"Do you have brothers or sisters?" Melody
asked unexpectedly. She hadn't ever had occasion to question his background. Now, suddenly, she was curious about it.

"No," he said. "I had a sister, they said,
but she died a few weeks after she was born.
There was just me. My dad was a rodeo star.
He taught me everything I know."

"He must have been good at it."

"So am I, when I'm not distracted. There

was a little commotion before my ride. I wasn't paying attention and it was almost fatal."

"The kids would have missed you."

"Maybe Guy would have, although he's pretty solitary most of the time," he replied. His eyes narrowed. "Amy and Polk seem very happy to stay with anybody."

So the truce was over. She stared at him. "They probably were half-starved for a little of the attention you give rodeoing," she returned abruptly. "You seem to spend your life avoiding your own children."

"You're outspoken," he said angrily.

"So are you."

His green eyes narrowed. "Not very worldly, though."

She wouldn't blush, she wouldn't blush, she wouldn't...!

"The eggs are getting cold," she reminded him.

The color in her face was noticeable now, but she was a trouper. He admired her attempt at subterfuge, even as he felt himself tensing with faint pleasure at her naiveté. Her obvious innocence excited him. "I have to make a living," he said, feeling oddly defensive. "Rodeo is what I do best, and it's profitable."

"Your cousin mentioned that the ranch is profitable, too."

"Only if it gets a boost in lean times from other capital, and times are pretty lean right now," he said shortly. "It's the kids' legacy. I can't afford to lose it."

"Yes, but there are other ways of making money besides rodeo. You must know a lot about how to manage cattle and horses and accounts."

"I do. But I like working for myself."

She stared pointedly at his head. "Yes, I can see how successful you are at it. Head not hurting this morning?"

"I haven't taken a fall that bad before," he muttered.

"You're getting older, though."

"Older! My God, I'm only in my thirties!"

"Emmett, you're so loud!" Amy protested sleepily from deep in her blankets.

"Sorry, honey," he said automatically. His green eyes narrowed and glittered on Melody. "I can ride as well as I ever did!"

"Am I arguing?" she asked in mock surprise.

He got up from his chair and towered over her. "Nobody tells me what to do."

"I wasn't," she replied pleasantly. "But when those kids reach their teens, do you really think anyone's going to be able to manage them? And what if something happens to you? What will become of them?"

She was asking questions he didn't like. He'd already started to ask them himself. He didn't like that, either. He went off toward the bedroom to call the boys and didn't say another word.

Melody worried at her own forwardness in mentioning such things to him. It was none of her business, but she was fond of Amy and Polk. Guy was a trial, but he was intelligent and he had grit. They were good kids. If Emmett woke up in time to take proper care of them, they'd be good adults. But they were heading for trouble without supervision.

Emmett came back wearing a checked shirt and black boots. Being fully dressed made him feel better armored to talk to Miss Bossy in the kitchen.

"They're getting up," he muttered, sitting.

"I'll warm everything when they get in here." She busied herself washing the dishes and cleaning the sink until the boys came out of her room, dressed. Then she escaped into the bedroom and closed the door. Emmett's stare had been provokingly intimate. She'd felt undressed in front of those knowing eyes and she wondered why he had suddenly become so disturbing to her.

Seeing him without his clothes had kindled something unfamiliar in her. She'd never been curious about men that way, even if she did daydream about love and marriage. But Emmett's powerful shoulders and hair-roughened chest and flat stomach and long, muscular legs, along with his blatant masculinity, stuck in her mind like a vivid oil painting that she couldn't cover up. He hadn't even had a white streak across his hips. That was oddly sensual. If he sunbathed, he must do it as he slept: without anything on. He looked very much like one of those marble statues she'd seen photographs of, but he was even more thrilling to look at. She reproached herself for that thought.

She looked at the rumpled bed where Emmett had lain with the boys and her pulse raced. Tonight she'd be sleeping where his body had rested. She wondered if she'd ever sleep again.

After she was dressed, she went to the kitchen and warmed the food before she put it on the table. The kids all ate hungrily, even Guy, although he wouldn't look at Melody. He was just as sullen and uncommunicative as ever.

But now, Melody was avoiding looking at him, too. Guy noticed her resentment and was surprised that it bothered him. He was guilty about the cat, as well. It had been an ugly cat, all scarred and big and orange, but it had purred when he petted it. His conscience stung him.

He had to remember that Melody was responsible for his mother's departure. He'd loved his mother. She'd gone away, so it had to be because of him. He'd given her a hard time, just as he'd been giving Melody one. He'd been much more caring about his father since his mother left, because he knew it was his fault that she'd run away with that Randy Cartman. If he'd been a better boy, a nicer boy, his mother would have stayed. Maybe if he could keep his father single, his mother would come back.

Blissfully unaware of his son's mistaken reasoning, Emmett smiled at the boy. He was a bit curious about Guy's behavior. The boy and Melody were restrained with each other. Melody's eyes were accusing, and Guy's were guilt-ridden. It wasn't a big jump from that observation to the subject of the cat.

He could ask Guy about it, but it would be better to let the boy bring it up himself, when they were away from here. If it was true that Guy really had let the cat out…

He was sorry that he'd spent so much time avoiding his children. Adell's betrayal wasn't their fault. If Adell genuinely loved Randy, and had left only because of that, no one was to blame for what had happened. Least of all the kids.

Emmett felt better about himself, and them. He had a lot of omissions to make up for, and he didn't know where to start.

The kids finished breakfast and went to watch television. Emmett insisted on helping Melody clean up.

He dried while she washed and rinsed. "Tell me about the cat," he said.

Her face stiffened.

"Come on." He prodded gently.

She sighed heavily. "I found him last year in an alley," she said finally. "He had a string tied around his neck. He was thick with parasites, and half-starved. It took him a long time to learn to trust me. I thought he never would." She washed the same plate twice. "We've been together ever since. I'll miss him."

"He may still turn up," he told her.

She shook her head sadly. "It isn't likely. There are so many streets…"

"If he was a street cat when you got him, he's street smart. Don't give up on him yet."

She smiled, but she didn't reply.

"What you said about the kids," he began, glancing toward the living room to make sure they weren't listening. "I guess maybe I've been negligent with them. I thought they were adjusting to my being away so much. But this concussion has made me apprehensive." He stared at her quietly. "Adell isn't likely to be able to handle all three of them with a step-father, even if she wouldn't mind visitation rights. They'd be split up, with no place to go."

"Adell loves them, you know she does," she replied.

"She gave up when I refused to let her see them. I never would have given up."

"Adell isn't you," she reminded him. "She isn't really a fighter."

"That's probably why she said yes when I proposed to her," he said angrily. "I was over-bearing, because I wanted her so much. If I'd given her a choice, she'd probably have turned me down."

"You have three fine children to show for your marriage," she said softly.

He looked down into her quiet dark eyes and something stirred deep inside his heart.

He began to smile. "You've been a surprise," he said absently.

"So have you," she replied.

He noticed that she'd thrown away a box of cat food. "Did you mean to do that?" he asked, lifting it.

She grimaced. "Well, he's gone, isn't he?" she asked huskily.

She turned to put away the plates and he moved, but she caught her foot on a chair leg and tripped.

He caught her easily, his reflexes honed by years of ranch work. His lean hands on her waist kindled exquisite little ripples on her skin. She looked up into his eyes and her gaze hung there, curious, a little surprised by the strength of the need she felt to be held close against him and comforted.

He seemed to understand that need in her eyes, because he reacted to it immediately. Taking the clean colorful plastic plates from her hand in a silence broken only by the blaring television, he set them on the table. Then he pulled her quite roughly into his arms.

She shivered with feeling. Never, she thought, never like this! She was frightened, but she didn't pull away. She let him hold her, closed her eyes and delighted in the security she felt for this brief moment. It made the ache in her heart subside. His shirt smelled of pleasant detergent and cologne, and it felt wonderful to be held so closely to his warm strength.

"The cat will show up," he said at her ear, his voice deep, soothing. "Don't lose heart."

She had to force herself to draw away from him. It was embarrassing to allow herself to be comforted. She was used to bearing things bravely.

She managed a wan smile. "Thanks," she said huskily.

He nodded. He picked up the plates and handed them back to her. "I'll get the kids packed," he said.

He moved out of the kitchen. He was disturbed and vaguely aroused. He didn't want to think about how his feelings had changed since his concussion. That could wait until he was more lucid and out of Melody's very disturbing presence.

Guy had noticed the embrace and he remarked on it when Emmett joined the children in the living room.

"Losing the cat upset her," Emmett said, and that explanation seemed to satisfy Guy. At the same time, the boy's face went a little paler.

Later, Emmett promised himself, he was

going to have to talk to Guy about that cat. He had some suspicions that he sincerely hoped were wrong.

He and Guy weren't close, although they got along well enough. But lately the boy was standoffish and seemed to not want affection from anyone. He bossed the other two around and when he wasn't doing that, he spent his time by himself. He didn't ask for anything, least of all attention. But as Emmett pondered that, he began to wonder if Guy's solitary leanings weren't because he was afraid to get attached. He'd lost his mother, whom he adored, to a stranger. Perhaps he was afraid of losing Emmett, too.

Emmett could have told him that people don't stop loving their children, whether or not they're divorced. He'd done his kids an injustice, probably, by not letting Adell near them. He began to rethink his entire position, and he didn't like what he saw. He'd been punishing everyone for Adell's defection. Perhaps he'd been punishing himself, as well. Melody had said some things that disturbed him. That might not be bad. It was time he came to grips with the past, and his kids. Fate had given him a second chance. He couldn't afford to waste it.

Chapter 4

It only took her reluctant houseguests a few minutes to pack and be ready to leave.

"You could stay another day if you need to," Melody told Emmett and her dark eyes were worried. "Concussions can be dangerous."

"Indeed they can," he said. "But the headache is gone and I'm not feeling disoriented anymore. Believe me, I don't take chances. I'm all right. I'd never take the kids with me if I wasn't sure."

"If you're sure then," she said.

"Besides," he added ruefully, "we've given you enough trouble. Thank you for taking care of those kids for me. And for your hospitality."

He opened his wallet and put two twenty-dollar bills on the table. "For groceries," he said.

"They didn't eat forty dollars' worth of food," she returned angrily.

"The babysitter cost that much for two hours, much less two days," he said, putting his wallet away. "I won't argue. I don't want to be under any obligation to you. In my place, you'd feel exactly the same," he added with a smile when she started to protest again.

She would have felt the same way, she had to admit. Reluctantly, she gave in. "All right. Thank you," she said stiffly. "I hope you'll be all right," she added. She couldn't quite hide her worry for him.

Her concern touched him. "I will. I've got the world's hardest head." He guided the kids out the door. "We'll get a cab," he added when she offered to drive them.

"I'll miss you, Melody," Amy said sadly. She hugged Melody warmly. "Can't you come with us?"

"I've got a job," Melody said simply. She smiled and kissed the little girl's forehead. "But I'll miss you, too. You could write me, if your dad doesn't mind."

"Me, too?" Polk asked.

She smiled. "You, too."

He beamed. Guy didn't say a word. He stuck his hands into the pockets of his jeans and trailed after Amy and Polk.

"I'll say goodbye, then," Emmett said quietly. He searched Melody's eyes, feeling oddly disconcerted at the thought of not seeing her again. He scowled, his expression steady and intent, and a jolt of pure pleasure seared through him as he let his gaze fall slowly to her mouth. It was silky and soft looking, and he wondered how it would feel to smooth her body against his and kiss her blind.

He dragged his gaze away. He must still be concussed, he decided, to be considering that! Any such thoughts were a road to disaster. She, of all women, was off-limits. He would never forget Adell and Randy. The past would destroy any thought of a relationship with Melody.

"Goodbye," he said stiffly, and followed the kids into the elevator. Guy looked over his shoulder, and there was something in his eyes that mingled strangely with the hostility. He looked as if he were about to say something, but Emmett's gentle hand on his shoulder guided him out the door.

The apartment was quiet and lonely with everyone gone. Melody got her clothes ready for work the next day, but she did it without any real interest. With a sinking heart, she washed Alistair's bowls and put them out of sight. Tears stung her eyes at the thought of never seeing him again. She'd never dreamed that a child could be so vindictive.

Back at the hotel, Guy was totally uncommunicative until that night. After Amy and Polk went to bed, he sat down on the couch next to his father.

"Something's bothering you," Emmett remarked quietly.

Guy shrugged. "Yeah."

"Want to tell me about it?"

The boy leaned forward, resting his elbows on his knees in a position that Emmett often assumed.

"I let Melody's cat out."

Emmett's head lifted. He wasn't really surprised. He'd suspected this because of Guy's behavior. "That was cruel," he replied, "after she was kind enough to take care of all three of you. The cat was special to her. Like Barney is to you," he added, mentioning the mongrel pup that Guy was fond of back home. "Try to think how you'd feel if someone let Barney out in the streets..."

Guy burst into tears. It was the first time in memory that Emmett had seen that happen. Even when his mother left, Guy hadn't cried.

Awkwardly Emmett pulled the boy against him and patted his back. He wasn't too good at being a parent most of the time. The kids made him uncomfortable with their woes and antics, which was really why he spent so much time away from home. Now he wondered if he'd been needed more than he realized. The kids hadn't had anyone to talk to about their mother in two years, or anybody to lean on. He'd assumed that they hadn't needed that. But they were only children. Why hadn't he realized how young they really were?

"Why did you let the cat out?" Emmett asked Guy gently.

"Because I hate her! She helped Mom leave!" Guy choked. "She's nothing but a troublemaking witch!" He looked up, a little uncertainly. "You called her that!" he added defensively, because his father didn't look pleased about what he'd said.

Emmett groaned. "Yes, I did, but it was because I was hurting. Nobody made your mother leave. She went away because she never really loved me." It was painful to say that, but now that it was out, it didn't hurt so much. "She did fall in love, but with another man, and she couldn't live without him. That's not your fault or mine or Melody's. It's just life."

Guy sniffed, and pulled away, wiping his tears on the back of his hand. "Melody cried all night. I heard her. I thought it would serve her right, because of Mom. But it made me feel awful."

"It made her feel pretty awful, too."

"I know." He looked up at his father. "What'll I do?"

Emmett thought for a minute. "Go to bed. I've got an idea. We'll talk some more tomorrow."

"We're going home, aren't we?"

"Yes. Tomorrow afternoon. But first, in the morning, I want to make a few phone calls."

He made eight phone calls before he got the information he wanted. His head had stopped throbbing and he felt much better. Leaving the kids with a babysitter—not the elderly one of two nights ago—he went downstairs and hailed a cab.

Melody was just hanging up the telephone when she heard the outer office door open. She looked up with a smile ready for the client coming in. But it wasn't a client; it was Emmett. And under his arm was a big, straggly-looking orange tabby cat.

"Alistair!"

She scrambled up from the desk, tears of joy streaming down her face. "Alistair! Oh, Alistair...!"

She took the cat from Emmett and kissed Alistair and hugged him and petted him and stroked him in such delight that Emmett felt even worse than he had when Guy told him what he'd done. Seeing Melody vulnerable like this touched him. It was as shocking as it had been to see Guy in tears.

"Where did you find him?" she choked, big-eyed.

He touched her cheek gently. "At the local pound," he said. He didn't add that the shelter had been in a state of chaos and the cat had inadvertently been scheduled for premature termination. That wouldn't do at all. "I suppose you know that it was Guy who let him out."

"I know," she said.

"It's my fault more than his," he murmured reluctantly. "I've blamed everyone for Adell, especially you. I couldn't stand to admit that she left because of me, because she didn't love me. I stayed away too much. The kids and the loneliness killed our marriage."

"Not the kids," she replied, clutching Alistair. "Adell loves the children. She'd love to have them visit, but…" She paused.

"But I wouldn't let her near them. That's right," he agreed tersely. "I hated her, too. Her, and your brother and you. Everybody."

"You were hurt," she said softly, her eyes searching his. "We all understood. Even Adell."

His jaw went taut. He took a deep breath and looked over her head. "We're flying out this afternoon. I have to go."

"Thank you for my cat," she said sincerely. In a fever of gratitude and without thinking of the consequences, she reached up and touched her soft lips fervently to his chin.

Shocked at the look it produced on his lean, dark face, and not a little by her own behavior, she drew back at once.

He looked down at her curiously, stunned. When she began to step away, his lean hand caught her shoulder and stopped the slow movement.

"No," he said hesitantly, searching her soft, dark eyes while his heart began to race in his chest. "Not yet, Melody."

While she was getting her breath, he let his gaze drop abruptly to her soft, parted mouth and his big hand moved up to her chin, gently cupping it as he tilted her face up.

His thumb moved hesitantly over her full lower lip. "I've…wondered," he whispered as his head began to lower. "Haven't you?"

She didn't get the chance to reply. His mouth slowly closed on hers with tender, confident mastery. It was firm, and hard and a little rough. She let her eyes close and stopped breathing. She'd been kissed, but just the touch of a man's lips had never been quite so vivid. It had to be because of the antagonism they'd felt for each other, she thought dizzily.

But her knees were going weak and her heartbeat went wild when she felt his teeth gently nip her lower lip. She heard his breathing change even as his head lifted a fraction of an inch.

"Open it," he said roughly, his hand sliding into the thick hair at her nape. "Open your mouth…!"

His lips crushed into hers with sudden violence, hunger making him less considerate of her needs and more aware of his own. With a rough groan, he made her lips part to admit his, and his tongue probed insistently between them.

Shocked, her gasp gave him what he wanted—

access to her mouth. He made a satisfied sound in his throat and penetrated the soft, warm darkness past her lips with slow thrusts.

She gasped and clutched at him as waves of physical pleasure buffeted her untried body. Her mouth pushed upward, to meet his ardor headlong. And Alistair chose that instant to insist physically on being put down, his claws digging into her arm.

She pulled away from Emmett, breathless and puzzled by the violence in his eyes. His hand let go of her hair. She looked away while she put the battle-scarred old tomcat on his feet and dazedly watched him leap into her chair and begin to bathe himself with magnificent abandon.

She took steadying breaths and slowly looked at Emmett. He seemed as shaken as she felt. Her dark eyes stared up into his turbulent green ones with mute curiosity.

The delight he felt was far too disturbing. He could get in over his head here with no trouble at all. The chemistry was there, just as he'd known it was somewhere in the back of his mind. He was sorry about that. Of all the women he'd ever wanted, Melody was the first one that he absolutely could not have.

He forced himself to breathe normally, to

pretend that it was natural for him to feel this aroused from a casual kiss. He had to force back the impulse to drag her against him.

He laughed a little angrily. "I'm glad the cat turned up," he said when he wanted to ask how she felt, if her body was throbbing as madly as his own was. He had to keep his head, talk normally. "Thanks for the hospitality."

"That's all right." She could barely speak. She cleared her throat. "Thank you for finding my cat. He…he really is all I have."

His throat felt tight. He had to stop looking at her mouth. His broad shoulders squared. "Guy's sorry for what he did. I'll make sure he doesn't do it again."

"You won't…be mean to him?"

He cocked an eyebrow. "I don't have a bull-whip."

She flushed. "Sorry," she said sheepishly.

He managed a short laugh. "I don't beat my kids. Can't you tell?"

She smiled at him, her lips still tingling with pleasure from the hunger of his mouth.

He smiled back. She looked delectable when she smiled. He wanted her. No! He couldn't afford to think like that.

"Well…goodbye."

"Goodbye," he said. He hesitated for an instant. She made him want things he'd forgotten he needed. There had been women, but this one touched him in ways no one else ever had. He wanted to tell her that, but he didn't dare. There was no future in a relationship between them. Surely she knew, too, that it had been an impulse, a mad moment that was better forgotten by both of them.

With a tip of his broad-brimmed hat, he turned abruptly and left without looking back.

Melody stroked her cat with a hand that trembled. "Oh, Alistair." She sighed, cuddling him. "I've missed you so much!"

Alistair butted his head against her and purred. She laughed, imagining that he was telling her he'd missed her, too. She murmured a small prayer of thanks and carried him into the bathroom. He'd have to stay there until it was time to go home. Perhaps she could find him part of a sandwich and a saucer of milk later to keep him happy.

Emmett was set upon the minute he walked into the hotel room.

"Did you find him?" Guy asked impatiently.

Emmett put off telling him long enough to make him sweat. Object lessons stayed in the mind. "Yes, I found him," he said, and watched the young face lose its pallor. "No thanks to you," he added firmly. "He was scheduled to be put down."

"I'm sorry," Guy said tightly. He was trying not to hope for too much. Last night, his father had been approachable for the first time in memory. It had felt good to be cared about. But now Emmett seemed distant again, and Guy was feeling the transition all too much.

Emmett turned away. He didn't see the wounded look on the young face, or the hope that slowly drained out of it. "You got a second chance. Most people don't. Remember how it felt. That way you won't be tempted to do such a cruel thing again."

"You hate her," Guy muttered. "You said you did," he added defensively.

"I know." Emmett hesitated. "I'll try to explain that one day," he told his son, and somewhere in the back of his mind he was remembering the incredible softness of Melody's innocent mouth under his lips.

He paid the babysitter, packed the suitcases and took his kids home. Maybe when he was back in familiar surroundings, he could put Melody out of his thoughts.

Melody checked on Tansy Deverell Sunday evening. Tansy had been discharged from the hospital and had been moved to Logan's house where she had a private nurse until Kit and Logan got back so that she wouldn't be in the house alone. Spending the evening with the elderly lady took her mind off her own problems.

"I saw Emmett before they released him," Tansy mused with twinkling eyes when she was in a comfortable bed at Logan's house. "Two nurses threatened to resign, I believe?"

"I heard it was three, and the doctor." Melody chuckled. "Isn't he something? And those kids…!"

"Those kids would settle down if Guy would," Tansy replied. "He's the ringleader. He leads and the other two follow. Guy's said the least about his mother leaving them, but I think it hit him the hardest—almost as hard as it hit Emmett. They both blame themselves, when it was no one's fault."

"I told Emmett that," Melody remarked. "He actually listened. I don't know if he believed me or not, but he was…well, less volatile after that."

"Emmett's always been explosive," the elderly woman recalled. "He was high-strung and forceful when he was younger, a real hell-raiser. Adell was sheltered and shy. He just walked right over her. He was devastated when his mother committed suicide and he wanted a wife and a family right then. He picked Adell and rushed her to the altar. She never should have married him. He was the exact opposite of the kind of man she needed. She didn't want a fistful of children right away, but Emmett gave her no real choice. He's lived to regret his rashness. I'm sorry for the way things turned out for him. He's a sad, lonely man."

"And a very bitter one," Melody added. "He hated me."

"Past tense?" Tansy fished gently.

"I don't know. He was very different when he left," she replied, frowning in confusion.

"I hope he'll go home and rethink his life after this," Tansy said. "He had a close call that could have ended tragically. The kids deserve a better shake than they're getting. If he doesn't wake up pretty soon, he'll never be able to control them when they get older."

"I think he knows that."

"Then let's both hope he'll do something about it. They're sweet kids."

Melody only nodded. She didn't want to go into any details about why she could have cheerfully excluded Guy from that description.

"It's great to be back." Kit sighed when she stopped by the office Monday morning with a weary-looking Logan. "You really need a vacation from a vacation. We had so much fun!" She stared after Logan, who'd gone into his office to take a telephone call.

Melody stared at her grimly. "I'm glad you did," she said, emphasizing the "you." "Emmett landed himself in the hospital with a concussion over the weekend. Guess who got to look after those kids."

"Oh, Lord," Kit said on a moan. "You poor thing!"

"I kept reminding myself that they're my nieces and nephews," Melody remarked. "But it was a very long weekend." She didn't mention Alistair's adventure or Guy's part in it.

"I'm really sorry. If we'd been in town, all of us could have split them up."

"I shudder to think of the consequences," Melody mused. "I can see them now, trying to get to each other through downtown Houston at two in the morning."

"Hmm. You might have a point there." She glanced at her watch. "I have to get to work, or I may not have a job. Have a nice day," she called, pausing to blow a kiss at her husband through the open door of his office.

Melody wondered at the obviously loving relationship the married couple had, and felt

a faint envy. Probably she'd never know anything like that. Emmett had kissed her, but it
had been passionate, not loving. She permit-
ted herself to dream for just a moment about
how it would have felt to be loved half to death.
Then the phone rang and saved her from any
more malingering.

During the time Logan and Kit had been
away, Melody hadn't been forced to call on
Tom Walker. That was a blessing. He strolled
into the office later on the day Logan came
back, a little curious, because he'd expected
to have someone to advise in Logan's absence.

"I suppose I had you buffaloed?" he mused
in a deep voice with a very faint crisp north-
western accent, his dark eyes twinkling as they
met Melody's. "That was just bad timing before, when Logan left town. I'd already had
a hell of a day. You caught the overflow. I'm
sorry if I've put you off financial advisors for
life." There was a faint query in his scrutiny.

"You haven't," Melody said, and smiled
back. "But we really didn't have anyone with
an emergency this time. Aren't you glad?"

"I guess so," he said wearily. "It's been a
long week. How was the honeymoon?" he

asked Logan, who joined them in the outer office.

"Nothing like it. Get married and find out for yourself," he said, chuckling as he shook Tom's hand.

The older man's face closed up. "Marriage is not for me," he said quietly. "I'm not suited for it. Besides, when would I have time for a wife?" he added with a mocking smile. "I work eighteen hours out of every twenty-four. In my spare time, I sleep."

"That will get old one day," Logan told him. He was obviously thinking about Kit and his heart was in his face. "Time can pass you by if you don't pay attention."

Tom turned away. "I've got a client due. I just wanted to stop by and welcome you back. I'll be in touch."

"Don't forget, we're having dinner with the Rowena Marshal people next Saturday at the Sheraton."

"How could I forget? Ms. Marshal herself phoned to remind me," he said with a nip in his tone. "After expressing outrage that her business partner had dared to approach us about changing their investments without her knowledge. If you recall, I was against taking their account in the first place. It's been nothing short of a headache. They should have used one firm, not split their investments between two. I tried to tell them that, too. Ms. Marshal wouldn't listen."

"Mrs. Marshal," Logan corrected.

"Are you sure? When would she find time for a husband and family?" Tom muttered. "That cosmetic company seems to keep her as occupied as investments keep me."

"She and her husband are divorced," Logan replied. "Or so I hear."

Tom didn't say a word, but one eyebrow went up. "Am I surprised? How could a mere man compete with the power and prestige of owning one of the Fortune 500 companies?"

"I'm sure there's more to it than that," Logan replied.

Tom shrugged. "There usually is. Well, we'll see what they want to do after we talk to them. If you want the account, you can have it with my blessing. Tell her that, would you?"

Logan chuckled. "What have I ever done to you?"

Tom shook his head. "See you."

Logan watched him leave with narrow, curious dark eyes. Tom was a real puzzle even to the people who knew him best. He had a feeling his friend and the lovely Mrs. Marshal were going to strike sparks off each other from the very beginning.

He turned to Melody, who was sorting files. "Anything that can't wait until tomorrow?" he mused.

"Why, no, sir," she said with a mischievous smile. "In fact, I think I can now run the office all by myself, advise clients on the best investments, speak to civic organizations..."

"I can call Emmett and tell him you miss having him and the kids at your apartment, and that you'd like him to come back," he suggested.

She stuck both arms up in the air over her head.

He chuckled and left to pick up Kit at her office.

Emmett was wondering if his age was beginning to affect him. He was noticing things about his kids that had escaped him for months. They didn't take regular baths. They didn't have new clothes. They didn't do their homework. They played really nasty jokes on people around the ranch.

"You haven't noticed much, have you?" the housekeeper, Tally Ray, remarked dryly. "I've done my best, but as they keep reminding me,

I don't have any real authority to order them around."

"We'll see about that," he began irritably.

"Why don't you see about that? Because I'm retiring. Here's my notice. I didn't mind doing housework, but I draw the line at being a part-time mother to three kids. I want to enjoy my golden years, if you please."

"But you've been here forever!" he protested.

"And that's why I'm leaving." She patted him on the shoulder. "One week is all you get, by the way. I hope you can find somebody stupid enough to replace me."

Emmett felt the world coming down on his shoulders. Now what was he going to do?

He phoned Tansy, supposedly to check on her progress, but really to get some much-needed advice.

"You're playing with fire, you know," Tansy told him. "Living on the edge is only for people with no real responsibilities. Those kids need you."

"So does the ranch. How can I keep it without additional capital?"

"Get a job that doesn't have the risks of rodeo."

"Where?" he asked belligerently.

"Take down this number."

She gave it to him and he jotted it down with a pencil. "What is it?"

"It's Ted Regan's number," she replied. "He still needs somebody to manage his ranch in Jacobsville while he's in Europe. It won't be a permanent job, but it would keep you going until you decide what else you'd like to do with your life."

"Jacobsville."

"That's right. It's a small town, but close enough to Houston that you could bring the kids to see me. You'd have time to spend with them. You'd have a second chance, Emmett."

He could use one, but he didn't want to admit it. "That's an idea." He didn't add that it was going to get him closer to Melody than San Antonio was. He didn't know why it exhilarated him to think of being close enough to see her when he liked, but it did.

"Call Ted and talk to him," Tansy suggested.

"I suppose it wouldn't hurt."

It didn't. Ted Regan knew Emmett's reputation in rodeo and he didn't need to ask for credentials or qualifications. He offered Emmett the job on the spot, at a regular salary that was twice what he was pulling down on the rodeo circuit.

"Besides, it may turn into a full-time job,"

Ted continued in his deep, Texas drawl. "My present manager just quit. I don't know if I can spread myself thin enough to manage the ranch and keep up with my purebred business. I'm buying and selling cattle like hotcakes. I haven't got time for the day-to-day routine of ranching."

That was what worried Emmett. If he left his own ranch, he'd have to let Whit manage it for him. Whit was good, but could he hold it together?

"We'll have to talk about that later, but I will think about the offer," Emmett promised. "And thanks, I'll take the job."

"I'm glad," Ted replied. "I know you'll do it right." He gave Emmett a date to report and concluded the fine points of the agreement.

When he hung up, Emmett called the kids together and sat down with them.

"We're going to move to Jacobsville and I'm going to manage a ranch there," he began.

Guy glared at his father with pale, angry eyes in a face as lean and strong as Emmett's. "Well, I'm not moving to Jacobsville," he said curtly. "I like it here."

Amy took her cue from her eldest brother, whose pale eyes dared her to go against him.

"Me, too," Amy said quickly, although not as belligerently. "I'm not going, either, Emmett!"

Emmett looked at Polk. Polk didn't say a word. He just looked at the other two, grinned and nodded.

Chapter 5

Only a week ago, Emmett might have lost his temper and said some unpleasant things to the kids. But he'd mellowed just a little since his concussion. He was sure he could handle the children's mutiny. He smiled smugly. It was just a matter of outsmarting them.

"There are horses there," he remarked. "Lots of horses. You could each have one of your own."

"We live on a ranch, Emmett," Amy reminded him. "We already have a horse each."

"There's the Astrodome in Houston," he added.

"There's the Alamo here," Guy said.

"And the place where they film all the movies, outside town," Polk added.

"All our friends are here," Amy wailed.

He was losing ground. He began to lose some self-confidence. "You can make new friends," he told them. "There are lots of kids in Jacobsville."

"We don't want new friends." Amy began to cry.

"Oh, stop that!" Emmett groaned. He glared at all three of them. "Listen, don't you want us to be a family?" he asked.

Amy stopped crying. Her eyes were red but they lifted bravely. "A family?" she echoed.

"Yes, a family!" He pushed back his unruly dark hair from his broad forehead. "I haven't been much of a father since your mother left us," he confessed curtly. "I want us to spend more time together. I want to be able to stay at home with you. If I take this job, I won't be away all the time at rodeos. I'll be home at night, all the time, and on weekends. We can do things together."

Guy stared at him warily. "You mean, things like going to movies and goofy golf and baseball games? Things like that?" he said slowly, hardly able to believe that his father actually might want to spend any time with them. That wasn't the impression he'd been giving since their mother had left.

"Yes," Emmett said. "And if you had problems that you needed to talk to me about, I'd be there."

"What about Mrs. Ray?"

"She's resigning," Emmett said sadly. "She says she's reached the age where she needs peace and quiet and flowers to grow. So we'd have to replace her even if we stay here."

Guy and Amy and Polk exchanged resigned glances. They didn't want the risk of a housekeeper they couldn't control. There was always that one chance in a million that their father might come up with someone they couldn't frighten or intimidate.

"Melody could stay with us, couldn't she?" Amy asked suddenly.

"Sure!" Polk agreed, beaming.

Guy's complexion went pale. He muttered something under his breath and got up and went to the window to stare out it. He knew for certain that Melody wouldn't want him around, even if she did like the other two. She'd never forgive him for what he'd done to her cat. Besides, he reminded himself forcibly, he didn't like her. It was her fault that he didn't have a mother anymore.

Emmett found the suggestion warming, if impractical. He'd done a lot of thinking about Melody himself. "Melody has a job," Emmett said. It surprised him that the kids found it so easy to picture Melody as part of their lives. It surprised him even more that he did, too.

"Jacobsville isn't very big, is it?" Guy asked without looking at his father. "There's not much to do there, I guess."

"You're old enough to start learning how to manage a ranch," Emmett told him. "You can come around with me and learn the ropes."

Guy's usually taciturn face brightened. He turned. "I could?"

"Yes." Emmett's eyes narrowed. "I'll have to turn things over to you one day," he added. "You might as well know one end of a rope from the other when the time comes."

Guy felt as if he'd been offered a new start with his father. It was a good feeling. Guy looked at his siblings. "I'll go," he said, his expression warning them that they'd better agree.

Amy and Polk stood close together. "I guess it would be nice to have you at home all the time, Emmett," Amy said softly. "It would be 'specially nice if you didn't have to ride any more mean horses."

"We don't want you to die, Dad," Polk agreed solemnly. "You're sort of all we've got."

Emmett's lean face hardened. "Maybe you're sort of all I've got, too. Ever think of it like that?"

Guy looked uncomfortable and Polk just smiled. But Amy slid onto his lap and hugged him. She looked up with soft, loving eyes. "I'm glad you're our daddy, Emmett," she said.

At that moment, so was he. Very, very glad.

It couldn't last, of course, all that peace and affection. They moved to Jacobsville and they hadn't been in the big sprawling ranch house two hours when the cook started screaming bloody murder and ran out of the house with her apron over her head.

"What's the matter?" Emmett called.

"There's a snake in the sink! There's a snake in the sink!"

"Oh, for God's sake, woman, what kind of snake is it?" Emmett grumbled absently, more concerned about the books he'd been going over than this gray-haired woman's hysterics over some small reptile.

"It's twenty feet long!"

"This is Texas," Emmett explained patiently. "There aren't any twenty-foot-long snakes here. You're thinking of boa constrictors and pythons. They come from the jungle."

"Hey, Dad, look what we found in the barn!" Guy called, grinning.

He came out with a huge black-and-white striped snake. It wasn't twenty feet long, but it was at least six.

"Aaaaahhhhhhhhh!" the cook screamed and started running again.

"Go put it back in the barn," Emmett told them.

"But it's just a king snake," Polk protested.

"And he's very friendly, Emmett," Amy agreed.

"Put it back in the barn or she'll never come back. I'll have to cook and we'll starve," he explained, gesturing toward the figure growing smaller in the distance. He scowled. "As it is, I'll have to run her to the ground in the truck. Never saw anyone run that fast!"

"Spoilsport," Guy muttered. He petted the snake, which didn't seem to mind being handled in the least. "Come on, Teddy. It's back to the corn bin for you, I guess. I had hoped we could let him sleep with us. In case there were any mice inside," he said, justifying his reply.

Emmett could see the woman's face if she

started to make up a bed and found the snake with its head on the pillow.

"Better not," he replied. "I'll load my pistol. If you see a mouse, I'll shoot it for you."

"The snake's a better bet, the way you shoot," Guy drawled.

Emmett glowered at him, but the boy just grinned. He and the other kids took the snake out to the barn. Half a mile down the road, Emmett caught up with the cook and part-time housekeeper, Mrs. Jenson. After swearing that the kids would never do any such thing again, he coaxed her into coming back and finishing those delicious salmon croquettes she'd started to make.

It was a hard adjustment, being home all the time. Emmett discovered that fatherhood wasn't something he could take for granted anymore. He had to work at it. All the problems the children had at school—problems that poor Mrs. Ray had handled before—were now dumped squarely in his lap.

Polk had a terrible time with fractions, and refused to do them at all in school. Amy had attitude problems and fought with her classmates. Guy was belligerent with his teachers and wouldn't mind spending hours and hours at in-school suspension. All these problems with teachers erupted in Emmett's face, now that he had sole charge of the children.

"Why can't you kids just go to school and get educated like other children do?" he asked. He had notes from three angry teachers in his hand, and he was waving them at the children while they watched television and pretended to listen.

"It's not my fault I can't do fractions. The teacher says I'm not mathematical," Polk said with a proud smile.

"And I have a bad attitude, on account of I don't have a mommy and my daddy is never home and I need discipline and attention," Amy said smartly.

That stung. Emmett brushed it off and tried to pretend he hadn't heard it. "What's your excuse?" Emmett asked Guy.

Guy shrugged. "Beats me. Mrs. Bartley seems to have trouble relating to me or something."

Emmett's eyes narrowed. "That wouldn't have anything to do with the mouse you stuck in her purse before lunch yesterday?"

"Awww, Dad, it was only a little mouse!"

"You have to stop that sort of thing," Emmett said firmly. "We need a little more discipline around here, I can see that right now."

"You bet, Emmett," Amy agreed readily. She propped her hands under her chin and stared at him. "He's right, isn't he, guys?" she asked her brothers.

"It isn't our fault that the educational system is in chaos," Polk reported. "We're just the innocent victims of bureaucracy."

Guy nodded. "That's right."

Emmett sat down and crossed his long legs. "Victims or not, I'll thank you to start minding your manners at school. Or I might just forget to pay the electric bill. How would you watch television then?" he concluded smugly.

Amy sighed. "Well, Emmett, I guess we'd just have to watch it by candlelight."

Melody had put the children and Emmett forcibly out of her mind several times over the weeks that followed. Christmas came and went. She exchanged cards and presents with Randy and Adell, but it was still a lonely time.

It disturbed her that she kept staring at dark-haired men because they looked a little like Emmett. Remembering how he'd kissed her before he went back to San Antonio didn't help her nerves, either. She seemed to walk around in a perpetual state of nervousness, jumping when people came into the office.

"You are a case," Kit said, shaking her head when Melody leaped back from the filing cabinet as she came into the office after work.

"Nerves," Melody agreed. "I have nerves. It comes from mollycoddling nervous investors all day. It's a wonder I haven't shaken my desk apart."

"Work is all it is, hmm?" Kit asked.

"Of course," Melody replied.

The dark-haired woman only smiled. "Have you heard that Emmett and the kids moved to Jacobsville?"

Melody stopped filing and stared at her. "They did?"

"Emmett's accident must have made him do some hard thinking about his life. He phoned Logan last night and said he's given up rodeo to manage Ted Regan's cattle ranch in Jacobsville."

"Has he sold his own ranch?"

"He hired a manager. I suppose he'll make more than enough to keep his own place going until the economy gets a bit better. Meanwhile, he's having plenty of time with his kids."

"They all need that," Melody replied. "Guy especially."

"You don't like Guy, do you?"

"I don't really dislike him. But he hates me.

He can't forget that I helped his mother leave. I can't say I blame him. Divorce is hard on little children."

"It's hard on any kind of children, even big ones," Kit replied. "Why don't you go home? I'll take over here until Logan's ready to leave."

"How nice of you!"

"Well, not really. I enjoy spending time with my husband. Since we both work at different jobs now, every second is precious."

Melody envied her that happiness, but she didn't mind an early night. She said so.

"You're doing a terrific job here," Kit said before she left. "We both appreciate you."

Melody grinned. "You're only saying that because I don't wear blouses cut to my knees or have a breathy voice."

"That, too." Kit chuckled.

Melody waved and went back to her lonely apartment. A telephone call from her brother shocked her speechless.

"You never phone me," she reminded Randy. "I even had to call you at Christmas. Is something wrong?"

"You know me pretty well, don't you? It's not that anything is wrong. It's just that…we have a sort of awkward situation," he began slowly.

"Randy?" she persisted.

There was an audible sigh. "I don't know how to tell you, and you can't tell anyone… especially not Logan or Tansy. Not yet."

"Why not?"

"Because if it gets back to Emmett, I don't know what we'll do!"

She was getting worried. "Randy, what is it?" she said proddingly.

"Well, it's like this. Adell's pregnant."

Melody remembered belatedly congratulating her brother, but the news was a complication that wasn't going to make things easier for Emmett and the kids. A new child in a mixed family always brought turmoil. It was a shame, too, when Emmett and the kids had just gotten settled into a new life in Jacobsville.

On the other hand, she was going to be an aunt again, and a real one this time, because Randy was her own blood. It would be his first child. She couldn't be sad about that. But she hurt for Emmett. It wasn't going to be easy for him to learn that his ex-wife was pregnant by the man who'd taken her from him. It was going to cause all sorts of problems.

Emmett stopped outside Logan's office and hesitated. He hadn't wanted to come here, but Melody was playing on his senses. He'd missed her. Christmas, even with the kids, had been oddly lonely for him this year. There was a hollow place inside him that a casual date couldn't fill any longer. He'd brooded over what to do about it, and he'd finally come to the conclusion that he needed to see Melody again, to make sure he wasn't overreacting to her.

He'd looked for days for an excuse to show up here. He'd finally found one, in the guise of letting Logan invest some money for him. But he hadn't telephoned first. He wanted to know if Melody was as attracted to him as he was to her. The element of surprise was going to tell him that.

He opened the door and walked in. She was typing at the computer. She didn't see him at first, not until he closed the door and the sound distracted her.

She looked up with her usual welcoming smile for clients, but it fell short when she saw the man in the gray suit and Stetson standing just inside the door.

"Emmett!" she said involuntarily.

The light in her eyes couldn't lie. Emmett smiled, because she was glad to see him and it showed. He liked the way she looked in that figure-hugging beige dress, with her long hair in a neat French braid and her dark eyes warm in her freckled face.

"Hello," he replied. He moved close to the desk, feeling his body throb, his heart race as he drank in the sight and scent of her from scant inches away. His voice dropped an octave involuntarily in reaction. "You look well."

"I am. I'm fine. How about you?" she asked worriedly.

"No more problems. I have a hard head," he replied. His eyes slid over her face and down to the mouth he'd possessed briefly so long ago. It made him hungry to remember how eager and willing she'd been.

"Emmett!"

The exclamation came from Logan, who'd walked out with a letter to find his cousin standing over his flustered secretary.

"Hello, Logan," Emmett said, extending a hand.

"You look prosperous," Logan murmured with a smile. "What brings you to Houston?"

"I needed some advice. I was about to make an appointment…"

"No need for that. I'm not busy right now. Come on in." He handed the letter to Melody and tried not to notice that her hands were trembling. Emmett obviously had a powerful effect on her.

"I wanted to see you about some investments," Emmett said when they were sitting in Logan's office.

"Imagine that," Logan said thoughtfully. "You said you didn't trust the stock market."

"I've changed," the other man replied doggedly.

"Indeed you have. How is it, being a full-time father?"

Emmett tossed his hat onto a nearby chair. "It's hell," he said flatly. "I get all the hassles now. I never realized how much trouble three little kids could be. In fact, they're never out of trouble."

"Now that you're home at night, that will change, I imagine," came the droll reply. "You've spent a lot of time avoiding them."

"You know why."

Logan nodded. "Yes, I do. Are you finding your way out of the pit, Emmett?" he asked kindly.

Emmett ran a lean hand through his thick, dark hair. "Maybe. I don't know. A lot of things have changed since I had the fall. Maybe I was looking at it all the wrong way."

"Divorce isn't easy on anyone," Logan said quietly. "It would kill me if Kit left me, for any reason. I don't know if I could take it if it was for another man."

"That's how I felt. I thought I loved Adell," he said heavily. "I really did. But now I'm not sure it wasn't just hurt pride."

"Having her run out in the middle of the night with the other man involved couldn't have helped."

"It didn't. I guess maybe I understand why she did it now, though. She isn't a fighter," he added, echoing the words Melody had spoken. "She probably figured I'd play on her sympathy and talk her out of it if I had the chance." He smiled faintly. "That's what would have happened. She never could stand up to me in a fight." He leaned back. "It's all water under the bridge. I have to go on living. So does she. I want to make some provisions for the kids, in case anything happens to me. That's really why I'm here. I've got a little spare cash and I want to put it where it can grow."

Logan considered it for a moment, his eyes

narrowed. "All right. I've got a few ideas. How long are you going to be in town?"

"Until tomorrow," came the surprising answer. "Mrs. Jenson is living in, so that she can watch the kids while I'm away. I…have a few other things to do while I'm in town."

"Where can I reach you?"

Emmett gave him the number at his hotel. "Until six," he said. "I may have plans for the evening."

"Oh," Logan said with a chuckle. "Confinement getting to you, is it? I gather the plans have something to do with a woman."

"Well, yes."

"From what I remember, the kids would make any sort of relationship impossible. I haven't forgotten that they were trying to take off the door of the bathroom when Kit and I were in there, at your ranch."

Emmett grinned at the darkly accusing stare. "So they did. Good thing the screwdriver was too big, wasn't it?"

Logan gave in to laughter. Emmett was as incorrigible as his kids.

He showed the other man out, but Emmett seemed strangely reluctant to leave. Perhaps he wanted to tell Melody something about the children, Logan decided, so he said his good-byes and went back into his office.

Melody was typing nonsense into the computer, because Emmett's stare made her too nervous to function.

"Is there something you needed to ask me?" she said finally, dark eyes lifting to his.

"Yes," he said with a husky laugh. "What are you doing for dinner?"

Doing for dinner. Doing for dinner. The words passed through her mind with very little effect. She stared at him blankly. The telephone rang loudly and she jumped, fumbling the receiver all over the desk before she finally got it to her ear and gave the correct response.

"I'll put you through to Mr. Deverell," she said breathlessly, and buzzed Logan to give the caller's identity.

When she put the receiver back down, she was still very visibly shaken.

Emmett had his Stetson by the brim and he was watching her with a half-amused look that glittered in his green eyes. "Looking for excuses not to go?" he asked softly.

"Oh, no!" she replied huskily. "But why?"

"Why not?"

Her pulse started to run away. She wanted to

refuse. She should. But somehow she couldn't. "I...what time?" she asked.

"Six."

"This isn't a good idea, you know," she said. "I'm still Randy's sister, and the past hasn't changed. Not at all."

He moved closer to the desk and his lean hand toyed with a notepad on its paper-littered surface. His pale green eyes searched her dark ones quietly. "That's true. Maybe I've changed. I enjoy your company. I want to take you out for a meal. That's all," he added flatly. "You won't have to fight me off over dessert and coffee."

She laughed nervously. "That was the last thought in my mind."

He didn't believe that. But she relaxed, and he felt glad that he'd said it. He didn't want to make her uneasy. She'd been too much on his mind lately and he wanted to find a way to purge her from it. Perhaps closer acquaintance would solve the problem for him. Often women who seemed nice weren't, and they couldn't keep up the act when a man took the time to get to know them.

Melody was relieved by his blunt statement. There had been a time or two when she had found herself having to talk her way out of a difficult situation.

"I'll see you at six, then," he said.

He stuck the Stetson back on his head and went to the door. He paused there and turned. "I'm rabidly old-fashioned in one respect. I like dresses."

She grinned impishly. "Yes, but how do you look in a dress?" she asked curiously.

His pale eyes splintered with good humor. "Wear what you damned well please, then," he mused. "See you later."

Melody owned one nice dress. It was black with a silvery draped bodice and spaghetti straps. It flattered her full-figured body without making her sexiness blatant. She coiled her hair around the top of her head and wore more makeup than usual. The final touch was high heels. Most men she dated were her height or shorter. But Emmett was very tall, and she could get away with wearing high heels when she went out with him. She liked the way she felt when she was dressed up; very feminine and sensuous.

Now, she wondered, why should she think of herself as sensuous? She had to douse that thought before Emmett read it in her face. She didn't want any complications.

He was prompt. The doorbell sounded exactly at six. She opened the door and there he was, very elegant in dark slacks and a white dinner jacket with a red carnation in the buttonhole of his lapel. The stark white contrasted handsomely with his lean, dark face and dark hair. He had on a cream-colored Stetson to set off the elegance.

"You look very nice," she said huskily.

"Stole my line," he mused, grinning at her. "Ready to go?"

"I'll just get my wrap and my purse."

She draped a black mantilla over her shoulders and picked up her small black crepe purse. She checked to make sure Alistair had water and cat food. He was curled up on the couch asleep, so she didn't disturb him.

Emmett waited while she locked the door before he took her hand in his and led her along the corridor.

If someone had told her that holding hands could be a powerful aphrodisiac she might have laughed, but with Emmett, it was. His lean, strong hand curled into her fingers with confident possession. Beside him she felt protected and unexpectedly feminine. She couldn't remember ever feeling that way with another date.

He saw her expression as he led her into the empty elevator and pushed the down button. He'd let go of her hand to do that. Now he leaned elegantly against the rail inside the elevator as it started to move and just watched her, registering the conflicting emotions that washed over her face.

The tension between them was chaotic. She could barely breathe as she met his eyes and felt her knees go weak.

"You look lovely," he said, his voice deep, his eyes faintly glittery. "Black provides a backdrop for all the color in your hair and your face." His eyes fell to her draped bodice and lingered there, making her feel shivery all over.

"How do you like Jacobsville, you and the children?" she asked quickly, hoping to distract him.

"What? Oh, so far, so good. It's no picnic, but I think we're all getting the hang of it. It's going to be the best thing that ever happened to the children," he added quietly. "I honestly didn't realize how much out of hand they'd gotten."

He looked broody for a minute, and Melody wondered if there wasn't more to it than that.

But before she could voice her opinions, the elevator door opened and they were on their way out.

He stopped, taking her hand back in his and holding it warmly while he searched her eyes. "I like it better like this. Don't you?" he asked softly, and he didn't smile. His eyes dropped to her mouth. "For now," he added, very gently.

Chapter 6

The cool air on her face felt good as they left the apartment house and walked down the street. Melody was still vibrating from the heady experience of being on a date with Emmett. He, on the other hand, seemed perfectly nonchalant. Her heart was racing like a mad thing while they walked, hand in hand.

He led her to the car and unlocked it, but when he partially opened her door, he stood still, so that she couldn't get past him. She was so close that she could smell his tangy cologne, feel the warm strength of his body. It made her react in an unexpected way, and she moved back against the car a little self-consciously.

"You're nervous of me. Why?" he asked.

She twisted her bag in her hands and laughed. "I'm not, really." She shrugged. "It's just that it's been a long time since I've been out for the evening."

He tilted her face up to his quiet eyes. His thumb smoothed against her chin and her full lower lip, making sensation after sensation wash over her. She wasn't fooling him. He read quite accurately her helpless physical response to him. Whatever else she was, she wasn't experienced. That was unique to a man who deliberately chose women for their sophistication and disinterest in involvement. Melody was different.

"That's the only reason?" he asked, probing softly.

She couldn't hide her expression quickly enough. "Well...maybe not the only one," she said demurely.

He smiled with pure delight. He bent and his lips brushed gently across her wide forehead. She smelled of soap and skin cream and floral cologne. The mingled scents appealed to his senses. "There's nothing to worry about," he said quietly. "Nothing at all." He moved away from her then, still good-natured. "I hope you like a smorgasbord of choices. This restaurant has international fare."

The change from tenderness to companionship was unsettling, but Melody managed the shift. "I love international fare," she said.

He opened the car door the rest of the way and helped her inside. All the way to the restaurant, the most intimate thing he discussed was the stock market and the state of the economy. By the time they disembarked, Melody could have been forgiven for thinking she'd dreamed that gentle kiss in the parking lot.

It wasn't a terribly ritzy place to eat. The food was very good and moderately priced, but Melody didn't have to worry if her clothes were good enough to wear to it. The thought made her smile.

Emmett cocked an eyebrow. "Private thoughts?"

"I was just glad that I'm properly dressed for this place, without being underdressed," she confessed on a laugh. "I don't have the wardrobe for those French restaurants where they don't even bother to put the prices on the menus."

He chuckled. "I've eaten in a couple of those," he replied. "I never felt very comfortable in them, though. My idea of a good lunch is a McDonald's hamburger."

"Good old Scottish cooking," she mused, tongue-in-cheek.

He laughed with her as he sampled his rare steak. "You're remarkably good-humored."

"Oh, I like laughter," she told him. "Life is too short to go around with a long face complaining about everything."

He studied her over a bite of nicely browned steak. "You manage to work for my cousin without complaints?"

"Well…not many," she said. "And he's my cousin, too, you know."

His eyes grew somber and they fell to his plate. "So he is."

"You look so remote." She hesitated. "Oh, I see. You were thinking that Adell was related to him by marriage, and she's still related to him because she's married to Randy—" She broke off, flushing.

He put down his fork. His appetite had gone. He'd thought he was getting over Adell's defection, but apparently the wounds were still open.

"I'm sorry," she said with a grimace. "I've ruined it all by bringing them up, haven't I?" She laid down her own fork. "It won't work,

Emmett," she said suddenly, without stopping to choose her words. "There are too many scars for us to be able to get along. You're never going to be able to forget about Randy and Adell." That was true—and he didn't even know what she did, either, about Adell being pregnant. She felt guilty.

He lifted his eyes to her face. It made him angry that she'd assumed that he was romantically interested in her. It made him more angry that he'd actually been thinking along those lines until she'd dragged Randy and Adell into the conversation.

He lashed out in frustration. "Aren't you taking too much for granted? My God, this was only a dinner invitation, not a proposal of marriage!" he said angrily. His eyes calmed. "Or is that what you thought I might be considering by asking you out?" He smiled at her embarrassment without humor. "Do I really seem the sort of man who can't wait to get married a second time?"

She had to force down the hopes she'd been nursing since his invitation to this meal. He obviously had cold feet about any relationship between them, and he was hiding it in sarcasm. She knew that as surely as if he'd told her so.

"Of course not," she lied. "That isn't what

I was thinking at all. I only meant that taking me out isn't a good idea."

"For once, we agree on something." He lifted his coffee cup to his firm lips, averting his gaze. He must have been out of his mind to have come up to Houston in the first place. Asking Melody out had been another temporary mental aberration. He had enough trouble already without rushing out to search for more.

"Are you finished?" he asked when he'd drained his cup.

She was glad she hadn't wanted dessert. He seemed to be in a flaming rush to leave. She was eager to oblige him. The evening had been an unmitigated disaster!

He drove her back to her apartment in a furious silence, without even tuning in a song on the radio to break the tension. Melody didn't feel any more inclined toward conversation than he seemed to.

She rode up in the elevator beside him without looking to the side. He paused at her door, sighing angrily.

"Thank you for an interesting evening," she said tightly.

"It was gratitude for keeping the kids," he said, his words as clipped as her own. "That's all. It was a belated thank-you for kindnesses rendered."

"And accepted in the same vein," she said. "No complications wanted."

"That's right, and you remember it," he said through his teeth. "You're the last damned complication I need right now!"

"Did I offer to be one?" she asked, aghast.

"Whether you did or not is beside the point! I've got kids who can't get along with anyone because they don't get any love at home. Their father doesn't give a damn about them and their mother ran away with your damned brother!"

The anger she'd felt was suddenly gone as she saw through the furious words to the hurt beneath it. He was wounded. She wondered if he knew how obvious it was, and decided that he didn't. Her dark eyes lost their glare and became gentle. She reached out with unexpected bravery and took one of his big, lean hands in hers.

"Come inside and have some coffee, Emmett," she said gently. "You can tell me all about it."

He must be daft. He kept telling himself he was as he let her lead him like a lamb into the softly lit kitchen.

He perched himself on her tallest stool and watched broodingly while she filled the coffeemaker and turned it on.

She sat down at the counter next to him, her mantilla and purse deposited on the kitchen table until she had time to move them.

"What's wrong with the children?" she asked.

He sighed heavily. "Polk won't try to do his math. Guy can't get along with his teacher. Amy can't get along with anybody, and her teacher sends me this damned note that says she doesn't get enough attention at home."

"And you're doing the best you can, only nobody knows it but you, and those words hurt."

He lifted narrowed, wounded eyes to hers. "Yes, it hurts," he said flatly. "I've done my best to provide for them. All I've had since Adell walked out is a housekeeper. Now, I'm trying to put things right, but I can't do it overnight!"

She smoothed her fingers gently over the backs of his strong, lean hands. "Why don't you write Amy's teacher a note and tell her that," she suggested. "Teachers don't read minds, you know. They have to be told about problems. They're people, too, just like you and me. They can make allowances, when they know the situation."

He relaxed. His tall, broad-shouldered form seemed to slump. "I'm tired," he said. "It's a shock. New surroundings, new people, a new job with more responsibilities than I've had in years and the kids on top of it. I guess I got snarled up in it all."

"It's perfectly understandable. Don't the kids like it better, having you home?"

"I don't know. Guy's still standoffish. I've tried to get him interested in things around the ranch, but he's shying away from me. He's not adjusting very well to school, because the teacher wants him to mind and he won't. He can't seem to conform, and his temper is his worst enemy. Amy and Polk aren't much better, but at least I can handle them when they're not driving school officials batty."

"Better them than you?" she teased.

He chuckled reluctantly. "Not really. I'll have to bone up on fractions and spend some time with Polk. Maybe I just haven't found the right tack with Guy yet. He likes ranching, but we don't have much in common outside it."

"Emmett, hasn't it occurred to you that these problems could be nothing more than pleas for attention?" she asked. "Randy and I used to get into all sorts of trouble when Dad got too wrapped up in Mother's illness to notice us. It's a child's nature to want to be loved, to have proof of that love."

"Not only a child's, Melody," he said unexpectedly. His eyes searched hers from much too close. "Even adults can go off the deep end when no one gives a damn about them."

"You know the kids love you."

"I know." His chest rose and fell heavily and his eyes grew intimate, holding hers for much longer than necessary, making her own pulse race.

"The, uh, the coffee's ready, I think," she said. Her voice sounded husky, even shaky. She dragged her eyes away from his and went to get the coffee.

She took down cups and saucers from the cabinet, and while she got the coffee service together, Emmett moved around the living room, restless and unsettled. His eyes searched out the books in her bookcase, the framed prints on the wall. He seemed to be noticing everything, taking inventory of her likes and dislikes.

He was thumbing through a volume of poetry when she put the coffee things on the dining-room table.

He put the book down and joined her at the table. She put cream and sugar into hers. He left his own black.

"I've got some cookies around here somewhere," she offered.

"No need. I don't have much of a sweet tooth," he said. He stared into his coffee. "How did you know?"

"Know what?"

He looked up with a rueful smile. "That I needed to talk about the kids."

"You picked a fight for no reason," she murmured dryly. "I used to have a friend in school who did the same thing. She never said what was bothering her. She picked fights until I made her tell me." She fingered the rim of her coffee cup. "Or maybe you didn't exactly pick a fight for no reason," she added sadly. "You aren't over Randy and Adell, really."

He moved restlessly in the chair. "It's going to take time."

Her eyes lifted to his. He didn't know that Adell was pregnant. How was she going to tell him? How could she tell him?

He saw that curious expression and scowled. "There's something," he said slowly. "Something you're holding back. What is it?"

She averted her gaze to the coffee cup. "Nothing."

"Now you sound like one of the kids." He moved her coffee cup out of her reach and caught her hand in his over the small table. "Out with it. You made me talk when I didn't want to. It's your turn."

"Emmett…"

He nodded reassuringly. "Come on."

She winced. Her big, dark eyes were full of sadness, sorrow. "Adell…is pregnant."

He didn't react at all for a minute. He let go of her hand and sat back in his chair. He let out a long, rough breath. "Well."

"You'd have found out sooner or later. I didn't want to have to be the one to tell you."

He looked at her. "You didn't? Why?" he asked, letting the shock of what he'd learned pass over him for the moment.

"You resent me enough already because of my brother," she said miserably.

His eyes searched her wan, sad face. "Do I?" he wondered aloud. It didn't feel like hatred. No, not at all.

He drained his coffee cup, and she took it, and hers, into the kitchen. She felt terrible. Working helped sometimes, so she busied herself loading the dishwasher. There wasn't much, but she'd saved last night's pots and pans to make a load. Behind her, she felt Emmett's eyes and could only imagine the torment he must be feeling. She wanted to console him, but she didn't know how.

After a minute, Emmett got up and poised himself against the kitchen counter to watch her work. He didn't want to think about Adell being pregnant by her new husband. He wasn't going to let himself do that now. Later would be time enough.

Melody was graceful for such a tall woman, he thought reluctantly, watching her hands as she put the dishes into the dishwasher.

She noticed the look she was getting. It made her tingle. He'd long since taken off his dinner jacket and tie and Stetson. His long-sleeved, pristine white shirt was partially unbuttoned and the sleeves were rolled up. He looked elegant and rakish, and Melody was surprised that he seemed to find her so interesting. He'd been married, and she knew very well that women still chased him. He had more experience than any man she'd ever dated. It made her nervous to remember how vulnerable she was with him, how easily he could overrule her and take anything he wanted. She hoped her unease didn't show too much.

"You're efficient," he remarked.

She smiled. "Oh, I'm very domestic. I had to learn early. My mother was an invalid for years before she and Dad died. Randy and I would have starved if I hadn't been able to cook."

His face closed up at the mention of his ex-wife's new husband.

Melody put detergent into the dishwasher and started it running. Her eyes flicked to Emmett and away. "Yes, I know, you hate my brother as much as you hate me."

His green eyes were completely without hostility for once as he studied her. The black dress she was wearing suited her fair complexion. Its fit emphasized her full breasts and hips and small waist, and the milky-white softness of her shoulders with their scattering of freckles. He liked what he saw when he looked at her, even if it was against his better judgment.

"I don't hate you," he said quietly.

"Pull the other one, Emmett."

She'd turned and was starting out the door when he moved with surprising speed and blocked her way. "I like the way you say my name. Say it again."

His arm was across the doorway, almost touching the tips of her breasts. She tensed at the sensual threat of it. "This isn't wise," she said seriously, meeting his green eyes levelly.

One eye narrowed. His gaze on her face was intent, curious. "Isn't it? Maybe not. We're years apart—almost a generation. Funny, I always thought you were older. I don't know why. You seem very mature for a woman just barely out of her teens."

"I had to grow up fast. May I get by, please?"

He could see her breathing quicken. "Why are you afraid of me?"

Her eyes darted up and down again. Her cheeks colored. "Am I?"

He reached out and caught her by the waist. He tugged, pulling her slowly to him, so that her mouth was poised just under his.

"Maybe intimidated is a better choice of words," he murmured. His hands slid up her rib cage with slow sensuality, making her flinch at the sudden pleasure of their touch. "I know a hell of a lot more than you do about this, don't I, little one?" His breath was warm on her parted lips. "Is that what's wrong?"

"Yes," she whispered breathlessly.

He looked at her mouth instead of her eyes. It trembled, pink and soft like some pastel flower, waiting to be touched. She was so young, he thought. She really was off-limits to a man his age.

But even as he thought it, his lips moved the scant inches necessary to bring them right down over her whispered gasp, and took possession of that petal-pink mouth.

She grasped his shirtfront and stiffened in surprise.

"Shh," he whispered against her lips while he worked with sensuous mastery at parting them. "You're safe. You're perfectly safe. There won't be anything to regret. Relax for me."

She'd been kissed. She'd been kissed plenty of times, and even by him! There was certainly no reason why Emmett's mouth should be so different from any other man's.

But, it was. Her whole body felt as if it contracted while Emmett's warm, strong arms enveloped her and his tongue slowly, tenderly impaled her mouth as it had once before. She stiffened again as the throbbing pleasure began to make her feel unwanted, unwelcome sensations. She fought them.

He felt the resistance, as slight as it was, and lifted his dark head.

"You're still holding back from me," he said, his voice tender if a little unsteady. "I'm not going to hurt you."

"It makes me feel funny," she replied dizzily.

His nose brushed lazily against hers. "Where?"

"In my stomach…"

"Good," he whispered. His lips eased back down and brushed hers apart, teasing them to make her mouth follow his in a sensual daze. His hands slid to her hips and contracted in a strangely arousing rhythm, pulling and pushing, brushing her legs against his.

She shivered. He felt that and lifted his head to search her wide, curious eyes.

"You're so young," he said quietly. He took a slow, steadying breath. "And so responsive that I'm likely to take advantage of it."

Desire had her in its grip. She wasn't afraid. She was hungry. "How?" she asked in a breathless whisper, and her eyes clung to his hard mouth as she spoke. "What will you do to me?"

His fingers eased up her rib cage and came to rest against the soft swell of her breasts. He nibbled at her mouth. One lean hand slowly cupped her and began to caress her with tender mastery. She started to stiffen until the dark delight of it made her go boneless in his embrace. She could have resisted his desire, but not her own. He was years beyond her in experience, and she reacted with helpless curiosity and need.

He nibbled tenderly at her lower lip. "I know. It's forbidden territory, isn't it?" he whispered into her parting lips. "Nice girls don't let men do this. Except that they do, Melody," he breathed as he drew her even closer. "This is part and parcel of being human." His thumb drew suddenly, tenderly, across her taut nipple, a fiery touch that caused her whole body to clench. Her nails bit into him and she gasped. "If I hurt you, I want to know it," he whispered. "Because it's only meant to arouse, not to bruise."

She shivered, but she didn't back away. She felt as if she had pulses where she'd never suspected, throbbing and hot. "It didn't hurt, Emmett," she admitted huskily, although she was too shy to look at him. She closed her eyes and hid them against his shirtfront. "Do it again."

He hadn't expected this kind of honesty, or as much cooperation. It ate at his control. His hand swallowed her, making magic on her body. She gave in without a sound, and he felt ten feet taller. He paused just long enough to unfasten his shirt halfway down his chest and drag her hand inside it, against the damp tangle of hair over the warm, hard muscles.

The feel of his body like that made her pulse throb. "You're hairy," she whispered.

"I'm like this all over," he whispered roughly. His hand moved down to her hips. The other one joined it. He pulled her into the blatant arousal of his body and held her there firmly but gently. "It's all right. Be still," he said when she tried unsuccessfully to pull away. He searched her face, finding shy curiosity there. "Have you never felt a man's body in full arousal before?"

"No," she managed to say, embarrassed.

"There's a first time for everything," he said softly, lowering his head. "I need oblivion and you need teaching. Think of it as a…reciprocal exchange."

"It isn't a good idea," she said unsteadily.

"I know. But it will be sweet."

And it was. The sweetest kind of exchange, savagely tender and violently arousing.

Her nails thrust gently into the hair at the back of his head while he kissed her and slowly caressed her breasts with hands that held a faint tremor at the license they were being given so generously.

In turn, she was learning about his body, enjoying the feel of the thick mat of hair over warm, firm muscles. She smoothed her hands sensually up and down his chest with delight while he taught her the intricacies of open-mouthed kissing. By the time he began to brush against her rhythmically with his hips, she was whimpering with the same desire that was riding him. But it couldn't go on. He was fast reaching the point of no return, and seducing her was impossible.

She felt swollen from head to toe, throbbing, when he finally lifted his head to look into her misty, half-closed eyes. He was more aroused than he could remember being in recent years. His body throbbed painfully with the need for release.

He pushed her hips away from his and took her face in his hands before he kissed her again, with growing tenderness.

She started to move closer, but he caught her by the waist and kept her away.

Her eyes asked the question that her swollen lips wouldn't form.

"Does the term 'playing with fire' ring any chimes?" he asked with forced, husky laughter.

"I don't care," she said unsteadily. Her face colored, but she didn't look away. "I like the way you feel."

His face tautened. "I like the way you feel, too, but a few minutes of feverish sex isn't going to improve our situation. And I did promise you that there would be nothing to regret." He forced himself to let her go and move away. He lit a cigarette. He hardly smoked these days, but he needed something to steady his nerves.

"A few minutes of feverish sex?" she said with a feeble attempt at humor as she leaned back against the counter and stared at him from a face that held lingering traces of desire.

He glanced at her and laughed, too. "Yes, well, it may be crude, but it was all I could think of at the time. I had to save you from yourself. Not to mention, from me." His eyes were bold on her breasts, assessing their taut peaks before his gaze lifted again to her flushed, excited face. "You're a quick study."

"Is that what I am?"

"That, and alarmingly innocent, for all your response just now," he added, the laughter leaving his eyes, to be replaced with quiet introspection. "Why are you still a virgin, Melody?"

She didn't bother to deny it. She knew all too well from what Kit had told her that he was definitely no novice. Women apparently fell over themselves trying to climb into bed with him. "I'm oversized and old-fashioned and plain, didn't you notice?" she asked, stung by the question.

"Don't take offense," he said quietly. "It wasn't a sarcastic question. If you want to know the truth," he added, his voice going sensual and soft, and his green eyes glittery, as he looked at her, "it excites me to the point of madness."

She drew a slow breath. "That's a new observation," she replied. "Most people think I'm crazy or fanatically careful. The truth is that nobody ever put on enough pressure to make me careless."

"Until now?" he asked gently.

She started to deny it, but that was pointless. He knew. She saw it in his eyes.

"Until now," she echoed.

He lifted the cigarette to his lips and blew out a faint cloud of smoke. Half angrily, he turned on the faucet and held the barely touched cigarette under it, extinguishing it. He tossed the finished remains into the trash can and stood staring down at it.

"I used to smoke a pack a day. I've lost my enthusiasm for it. Addiction is unwise." He turned and stared at her intently. "Any kind of addiction."

"Smoking is bad for you. I never even tried it."

"Good for you." He took the almost full

package out of his pocket and dropped that into the trash can, too. "I have to go."

She didn't want that. She felt a sudden, acute sense of loss that was puzzling.

She moved out of the kitchen and preceded him to the front door. But when she would have opened it, his big, lean hand flattened on its surface and prevented her.

"What are you doing Sunday?" he asked abruptly, and against his better judgment.

Chapter 7

Melody felt the floor giving way under her feet, and realized that it was because her heart was beating so fast. For a minute she thought he might be joking. But he didn't look as if he were, and there was a new softness in his green eyes.

"Why?" Her voice sounded like a croak.

He'd buttoned his shirt and put his dinner jacket back on. He finished with his tie and picked up his Stetson before he answered her. "I want you to spend the day with us so that I can show you the ranch," he said quietly. "Amy and Polk have talked about you since we left here. They actually asked if you could come and look after them when our housekeeper quit in San Antonio," he added with a smile. "They think you're great."

"I think they're great, too." She hesitated. "I'd love to. But Guy wouldn't like it."

"I know," he said easily. "Guy's been distrustful of everyone since his mother left." He grimaced, remembering what she'd told him about Adell. "I wouldn't dare tell him she's pregnant—him or the other kids. Not until I have time to prepare them."

"They'll adjust," she said softly. "It's amazing what people, even little people, can do when they have to."

"I guess so." He searched her dark eyes for a long time and laughed softly. "I hated you that night you helped Adell meet Randy at the airport to leave me," he recalled. "I said some terrible things to you. I guess I scared you pretty good, too, when I went after Randy." He shifted restlessly. "I'm sorry."

The belated apology was unexpected, as was the invitation to Jacobsville.

"People in pain lash out," she said simply. "I understood."

"All the same, you backed away from me when I first came to town with the kids."

"Self-protection," she mused. "Survival instinct."

"Yes, well I notice that it's done a nosedive tonight," he murmured, letting his eyes fall to the wrinkled black fabric of her bodice that his exploring hands had disturbed.

She cleared her throat. "What time Sunday?"

"I'll pick you up about ten. Or do you go to church?"

"I do, usually. But I'll play hooky Sunday. I could drive down," she added.

"I hate the idea of having you on the roads alone," he said. "It's a good long drive from Jacobsville to Houston."

She smiled. He was being protective. She didn't mind one bit. It was nice to be cared about, to have someone worry about her welfare. These days, that was unusual.

"Okay," she said gently.

His chest rose and fell heavily. He smiled back at her. "Can you ride?"

"A little."

"Play checkers?"

She blew on her nails and buffed them on her dress. "World champion class," she informed him.

He lifted an eyebrow. "Well, we'll see about that!"

She grinned. "Okay." Her eyes narrowed. "You'll be sure you take matches and ropes away from those kids before I get there?"

"I'll confiscate everything incendiary," he swore, hand over his heart. "Also sharp objects, blunt instruments and listening devices."

"They sound like a renegade branch of the CIA."

He leaned close. "They are. Juvenile division."

She laughed delightedly. "They're good kids, Emmett," she said. "All three of them."

"Guy was honestly sorry about the cat," he said with emphasis. "He's never done cruel things. Mischievous, yes, but they always drew the line at deliberately hurting people. He learned something from it."

"I'm glad."

"Sunday, then?"

She nodded. Her eyes sketched his face with soft hunger. He returned the look, but he didn't touch her again. It was a wrench, because he wanted to. The feel of her body in his hands had made him weak-kneed. His eyes slowly dragged over her and he felt himself going taut.

He had to get out of here before he did something stupid.

"I have to go. Good night," he said softly.

"Good night."

He opened the door and turned, silhouetted in the hall light. "Wear jeans and boots," he cautioned. "If we go riding, it's safer."

"I'll remember."

He winked at her, producing an odd jerky sensation in the region of her heart. Then he tipped his Stetson down over his thick, dark hair and walked away, whistling to himself.

Melody closed the door reluctantly. She could have stood watching him all the way to the elevator with the greatest pleasure.

Amy and Polk had been looking forward to Melody's visit all week. When she drove up with Emmett, they opened her car door and ran into her arms, laughing and talking together. Guy didn't move off the porch. He stood there, a little belligerent, with his hands tight in his jeans pockets, glaring.

Melody noticed him there, and thought how like his father he looked. It wounded her that she and Guy were enemies. It was going to make any relationship she tried to form with Emmett impossible. Emmett probably knew it, too, she thought. But perhaps friendship was all he had in mind. Then she remembered the way he'd kissed her and what he'd said about her innocence. No. Friendship wouldn't be all of it.

Fielding Amy and Polk, Emmett opened the door for all of them. Mrs. Jenson, looking harassed, stayed just long enough to meet Melody and then beat a hasty retreat to the kitchen.

"What did you do, try to tie her to the television?" Emmett asked his angelic brood.

"Not at all, Emmett," Amy assured him, smiling up at them. "Melody, how do you like our new house?"

"It's very nice, Amy," Melody replied. "Hello, Guy," she added coolly.

Guy only shrugged and didn't look at her.

He pretended to be watching television intently while Polk and Amy showed Melody all their treasures and school papers. Just as if she was already their mother, he thought bitterly. Well, he wasn't going to show her anything of his! Melody hated him, and he certainly hated her. She wasn't his mother. She wasn't ever going to be!

He glanced at her from his pale eyes, and his mind began working. It wasn't certain yet. He had time. He had to remember that, and not panic because his father had brought her down to the ranch. He could get her right out of his father's life if he just kept his head. The one thing he couldn't afford to do was let things get serious between them. His mother would come back one day. She'd get tired of her new husband and come home, and they'd all be a family again. Guy was sure of it. He just had to stop his father from getting involved with any other woman until that happened. And he would, too.

Melody was blissfully unaware of Guy's plotting, and frankly glad when he wandered off later to play with his dog, Barney.

"We can go riding after lunch, if you like," Emmett said, smiling at her while Amy and Polk turned their attention back to a nature special on television.

"I'd like that."

"Come on. I'll show you my horses." He held out his hand. She put hers into it, tingling at the contact. He looked good, she thought, in jeans and a blue-checked shirt and boots. He was tall and lean and she loved looking at him, touching him.

He was doing some looking of his own. She was wearing yellow jeans and a matching yellow knit sweater that suited her fair complexion. She walked just in front of him toward the front porch and his eyes narrowed on the fit of those jeans. He had to do some quick mental exercises to stop the physical reaction his interest provoked.

"It's beautiful here," she said, gazing lovingly around at the long, bare horizon and the white-fenced acreage thick with red-coated cattle. There were live oak and pecan trees all around the house, along with pines and thick glossy-leaved bushes.

"I guess it is. I miss my own place." He stuck his hands into his pockets and stared out at the barn. "I guess this place will be lush and green when spring comes. Right now, it looks a bit barren. And there's no mesquite," he muttered.

"Don't tell me you miss the thorns on the mesquite," she teased.

The light in her face made him hungry for things he didn't realize he wanted. He took his hands out of his pockets and captured one of her hands in his. "Come on and see the horses."

"Okay!"

He smiled and led her out to the barn. A small calf was resting in a stall by himself. Emmett explained that the calf's mother had died and he was malnourished before he'd been found. They were feeding him up before they went through the process of trying to pair him with a foster mother.

Down the aisle from the calf in a separate section of the huge barn, he had several saddle horses and a stud Appaloosa stallion in separate quarters. The stallion wasn't kept with the other horses. Emmett explained that it was because he was too volatile.

"I love Apps," he said wistfully, gazing at the big animal, which was mostly splashy red with white spots. "They're beautiful, but they have unpredictable qualities."

"Just like people," she teased.

He glanced down at her from under the wide brim of his gray working hat. "Just like people," he agreed. He let his eyes run down her body boldly. "You bother me in tight jeans. I didn't know you were going to look so sexy."

She laughed self-consciously. "Well, I never," she murmured.

"I know you've never," he murmured dryly. "That's another thing that excites me."

"You'll turn my head if you aren't careful," she said, trying to lighten the atmosphere.

"I'm tired of being careful." He drew up a booted foot and rested it on the lowest rung of a gate. "In between work and more work, you're all I think about lately," he said matter-of-factly, watching her with glittery green eyes. "I don't look at other women. I haven't slept with anyone since long before I got thrown off that bronc."

She was almost afraid to ask, but she had to know. "Because of...me?"

He nodded slowly. "Because of you." He sighed heavily. "Melody, you're barely twenty. It's a hell of a jump from your age to mine, and I've got a built-in family. I can't seduce you because my conscience won't let me. I can't stay away from you because you're obsessing me. Know that old saying about being caught between a rock and a hard place? I don't have any trouble understanding it these days."

She met his eyes steadily. "You want to sleep with me."

He frowned slightly, his expression whimsical. "I hadn't thought about sleeping, exactly," he said meaningfully. He scowled and his eyes narrowed thoughtfully. "On the other hand, I wouldn't mind holding you all night in my arms. I haven't wanted to do that since I was courting Adell." He pushed his hat back from his forehead, and his level stare didn't waver. "In fact, to be brutally frank, what I wanted to do with Adell was pretty limited. It's…different with you."

That was nice. She began to smile. She felt a delicious kindling of joy deep inside herself. He had to care a little, for there to be a difference. She wanted him, too, but it was much more than a physical need. The thought of lying close in his arms all night gave her a warm, comforting sort of pleasure.

"You don't wear pajamas," she said absently.

His eyebrows went up.

She flushed, remembering how he looked without clothes. "Sorry! I guess my mind was wandering."

"Oh? Where was it wandering?"

She traced the grain of the wood on the gate. "I was thinking about sleeping with you," she said quietly. "I haven't been held in a long time. Not…by anyone who cared about me."

"Neither have I."

She glanced at him. "Oh?" she said with a cold, speaking look, because she'd heard about the rodeo groupies of the past year.

His broad shoulders lifted and fell. "Being held in a sexual frenzy isn't the same." He scowled. "And I think there has to be more to a marriage than good sex. That's new for me.

Adell and I had nothing in common except desire and a love of children."

"That's pretty important, isn't it?" she asked.

"Yes. But common interests, mutual respect—those things make a relationship last." He smiled wistfully, studying her. "Funny, I could never talk to Adell the way I can to you. She liked sex, but she was ice-cold in the daylight, as if it embarrassed her that she had physical needs."

"I think a lot of women are like that," she said.

He tilted her chin up. "Are you going to be?" he asked, smiling indulgently. "Will you want the lights out the first time?"

She considered that. "I haven't let anybody see me without my clothes, except my doctor," she said. "I think it will be embarrassing, and I'll be self-conscious, because I'm big and a little overweight…"

He touched her mouth with a lean forefinger. He wasn't smiling. "You aren't overweight or oversized. You look like a woman should," he said. "I don't know why you think men should go lusting after skin and bones. There are exceptions, but most of us like a well-rounded figure with big breasts."

She flushed, but he wouldn't let her look away.

"Don't be embarrassed," he said gently. "There's nothing wrong with you. Nothing at all."

"Thanks," she said huskily. It was unusual to feel smaller than an Amazon. She smiled at him. Her eyes turned toward the doors of the barn, toward the outside, which was sun-lit and peaceful. "It must be nice to live on a ranch," she said with unconscious wistfulness. "I know it's hard work, but you're so far away from technology."

He laughed uproariously.

"What's so funny?"

"Wait until you see the mainframe computer in my office," he mused dryly. "Not to mention the state-of-the-art jet printer, the fax machine, the color hand scanner, the photocopier and the modem."

She stared at him blankly.

"I have to buy and sell cattle, keep up with sales reports, tally information about the herds and the cross-breeding program. I'm in constant contact with breeders and buyers, the National Cattlemen's Association, the Texas branch of it, not to mention veterinarians and state officials—"

"But you raise cattle, don't you?" she faltered.

"Raising cattle is big business these days,

honey," he said, the endearment, which he never used, coming so naturally with her that he hardly noticed he'd said it.

She noticed, though. Her face colored and her eyes brightened.

He touched her hair, fingering its thick, elegant length in the French plait. He wondered how it would feel to run his fingers through its thick, loosened strands at night. She didn't usually wear it down. "Honey," he repeated. "It's an endearment that suits you. Your hair looks like wildflower honey in spots, all golden and glowing in the sunlight, Melody."

As he spoke, he moved closer and his head began to bend. He brushed his mouth over hers until he coaxed it to open. Then he kissed her with piercing hunger, with possession.

Seconds later, she was riveted to every inch of him, held so close that she could feel him in an intimacy they'd only shared once before.

"God!" He ground out the single word, and his hand slipped under her yellow knit sweater to raid her soft femininity. He kissed her hungrily for a long few seconds and then lifted his head to look into her dazed eyes while his hand felt for the catch to her bra and snapped it with practiced efficiency.

He glanced around them to make sure

they weren't being observed. Then, while he watched her, his hand moved up to softly caress her bare breast. He felt it swell, felt its tip go hard and hot in his damp palm.

"Your breasts are very full," he whispered huskily. "I love touching them like this."

"Emmett," she protested weakly, and hid her face against his chest.

She was shy, but not at all inhibited or coquettish. He loved that honesty. His lean hand covered her completely, and he searched for her mouth until he found it.

She felt hot all over. Shaky. Throbbing with a kind of fever. She moaned faintly.

"Yes," he said roughly. "It isn't enough, is it?"

His hands went to the hem of the sweater and abruptly pushed it up, along with her loose bra. Then he stood and stared at her with an expression she'd never seen on a man's face before. She blushed, because certainly no man had ever looked at her bare breasts before.

"Baby," he said unsteadily, "you are a walking, blushing work of art!"

He made her feel beautiful. She watched him watching her and couldn't manage to feel any embarrassment. His eyes were explicit and very, very flattering.

His hands shook as he forced himself to pull the fabric down. He couldn't be sure those kids weren't hiding out somewhere nearby and he could lose his head much too easily if he did what he wanted to.

Her misty eyes asked a question.

He avoided meeting them while he reached behind her and refastened the bra under the cover of her sweater.

"I don't have a lot of control with you," he confessed quietly. "I don't want to push my luck and spoil things."

"You only looked at me," she whispered.

"That wasn't all I wanted to do, though," he said bluntly. He met her eyes. "I wanted to put my mouth on your breasts and taste you with my tongue and my teeth. And if I'd done that, I'd have taken you standing up, right here."

She stared at him blankly. "You would…bite me?" she asked uncertainly.

He laughed at her expression. "Not like that, for God's sake! I'd nibble you." He shook his head, because she so obviously didn't understand. "Melody, you're incredible. Just incredible. Have you done anything with a man beyond kissing him?"

She glowered at him. "Does it matter?"

"Yes, it does. I don't want to scare you."

"Did I act scared?" she asked, big-eyed.

He smiled, delighted. "No."

"I'm not afraid of you. I'm a little intimidated because I've never felt anything so overpowering before. But I enjoy having you touch me." She lowered her eyes to his broad chest. "I...would like to make love to you, Emmett."

He didn't say anything. After a minute, she was horrified that she'd gone too far, said too much, been too blatant.

She started to turn away, but he caught her softly rounded chin and turned her face back to his.

"I want that, too," he said tautly. "And that complicates things royally. I have three children. You might have noticed...?"

"They're pretty hard to miss," she agreed.

"And then there's the very obvious fact of your virginity." He brushed at his jeans. "Listen, I know it isn't modern or sophisticated, but I was raised to think of innocence as something too special to make an entertainment of. Do you understand? My parents always said that a decent man didn't make a plaything of an innocent woman, not when there were so many around who knew the score and weren't looking for marriage. But if a man seduced a virgin, he married her and made her the mother of his children. I'm afraid I still feel that way. I don't sleep with women who aren't experienced. Not ever."

"I see." She shivered a little, wrapping her arms around her chest. He was telling her that they had no future. She'd hoped. How she'd hoped! But she had to retain as much of her pride as she could. She forced a smile. "Well, no harm done. Do you think we could have some coffee?"

He felt her pain as if it had been his own. Amazing, he thought, that she cared so much that his words could wound her. He discovered that he couldn't bear to hurt her.

He pulled her into his arms and held her, feeling her stiff posture. He knew what to do about that. His hand slid sensuously down to her hips and moved her against him in a slow, sweet rotation.

She tried to move away, but he wouldn't let her.

"This hasn't happened with anyone since I first found you working in Logan's office," he whispered at her ear. "Do you feel how capable I am right now? I don't even have to work up to wanting you. I touch you, and I can take you. You'd have to be a man to appreciate how sweet that immediate response is."

"You just got through saying…"

"That I don't sleep with virgins," he finished for her. He smiled against her forehead. "That's right. Why don't you rip my shirt open and kiss me to death? You could push me down in the aisle here and ravish me, if you liked."

"Emmett," she said uncertainly, lifting her face to his.

"I'll get something to use the first few months," he said matter-of-factly, "so that you have plenty of time to decide whether or not you want to let me make you pregnant."

She stopped breathing. Her eyes went wide and shocked, and her heart began beating against her rib cage. "Wh-what?"

"Three is probably too many already," he murmured. "And the world is certainly over-populated. But I would love to give you a baby," he whispered. "I may not be the best father around, and I've got a lot to learn, but I love kids. We could have just one together, with honey-brown hair," he added thoughtfully, studying her. "That would be unique. Wouldn't you like to touch me?" he added huskily, dragging her hand to his chest. "I'd like it."

"Emmett, I can't get pregnant!"

"Yes, you can," he said. "It's easy. All we

have to do is not use anything when we make love." He lifted his head and frowned down at her. "Didn't you take health classes in school?"

"That's not what I meant! I can't go around getting pregnant!"

"You can if you're married," he reminded her.

"I'm not married!"

"You will be." He bent his head and kissed her, slowly and with a deepening hunger. "I can't wait long, either," he said unsteadily. "Some men can go for months without sex, but I can't. I have to have it. I've abstained since just before Kit and Logan got married, when I first realized that I wanted you. But it's been a long, dry spell, Melody." He moaned against her mouth. His hands became insistent. "Very long."

She melted into him. It wasn't a conscious decision, but she wanted him so badly that she couldn't manage any reasons to tell him she wouldn't marry him. The kids, the consequences, all took a backseat to his throbbing need and her desperation to satisfy it.

"I'll marry you," she said huskily. "I'm probably crazy, and I know you are, and I don't know how I'll manage being a mother to three kids when one of them hates me. But I guess

I'll cope, if you're actually proposing and not kidding around."

He lifted his head and searched her eyes. His hands on her hips were firm and bold. He ground her belly into his in blatant need. "Does it feel like I'm joking?" he asked unsteadily.

"No."

He brushed her lips with his and whispered something so explicit that she flushed and buried her face in his hot throat.

"Shocked that I can talk to you that way?" he asked roughly. "I'll make you like it, though. I'll make you like what I was talking about, too."

She pressed closer. Her legs trembled. "I know that," she breathed.

His head lifted. He searched her eyes. "Once you agree, there won't be any going back."

"No."

"Okay, then. We'll go and tell the kids."

"Not yet," she pleaded. "Not for at least a week or two. I want you to be sure, Emmett."

"I already am," he said quietly. It was quick, maybe too quick, but he didn't have a thought of hesitating. What he knew about her was more than enough. They'd have a good life together. He cared for her and he knew it was mutual.

"For the children," she hedged. "Let's give them a little time. Just a little, to get used to seeing us together, and doing things with them, before we hit them with it."

He groaned. "How much do you think I can stand?"

She smiled gently. "I'll be very careful not to make it any worse for you than it is."

He sighed roughly. "All right. But just a week or two."

She nodded. "That's fine."

Chapter 8

Melody went through the next two weeks in a kind of daze. She'd never felt as close to any-one as she felt toward Emmett and Amy and Polk. They went riding and to movies and ball games. They went to rodeos. They watched new releases on the VCR at her apartment and on his at the ranch. All the while, they grew closer as they talked about themselves and their hopes and dreams.

There was nothing physical. Emmett was restrained to the point of madness, only kiss-ing her lightly when he took her home. He never deepened the kisses or touched her or made suggestive remarks. Except for the way he looked at her now, they might have been nothing more than friends.

The one sadness Melody had was that Guy was more withdrawn than ever, and she couldn't help but think he was plotting against them. Amy and Polk had looked worried a time or two, as if they had something on their minds. Melody was tempted to try to pry it out of them, but there was never an opportunity.

Guy did find one way to irritate her. He found every photograph he had of his mother and put them all in plain view. He talked about Adell at every opportunity. Behind the irritating behavior was fear, but it didn't help Melody to know it. Guy had become her enemy, and she didn't know how to deal with him.

"You aren't giving Melody a chance, are you?" Emmett asked Guy late one evening after he'd taken Melody home and Amy and Polk had gone to bed.

Guy didn't look at him. "I thought you still loved my mother."

He frowned. "What?"

Guy shifted on the chair. "You were real mad when she went away, but you used to talk about her all the time. I know you miss her. So do we." He looked up at his father. "Why don't you tell her you want her to come back? She might. Maybe she doesn't like her husband. Maybe she'd like a reason to come back!"

Emmett couldn't tell him about Adell's pregnancy. It would be the last straw for the boy right now. He grimaced. He hadn't known that Guy was nursing such futile hopes. No wonder he was resentful of Melody and upset about her being around all the time.

"Son," he began slowly, "you have to understand that sometimes even people who care about each other can't live together."

"But you and my mother did," Guy returned. "You were happy, I know you were!"

That was desperation. Guy was growing up so fast, Emmett wasn't sure how to handle it. All that rodeoing, when his kids had needed him and he'd turned away from them, was coming back to haunt him now.

"Your mother wasn't happy with me," Emmett said quietly. "That's the root of the whole matter. She loves Randy," he added, gritting his teeth as he made the grudging admission. "There is no chance, whatsoever, that she'll ever divorce him and come back to us. You have to accept that."

"No!" Guy stood up. "She's my mother! She didn't want to go, you made her! You were never home!"

Emmett tightened the rein on his temper. "That's true," he said quietly. "Maybe my actions helped her make the decision. But the fact is, if she'd loved me, she'd never have left me. You don't run away from people you love."

Guy's lower lip trembled. "She didn't love me?"

"Not you! Me!"

Guy averted his eyes. "I don't like Melody. Does she have to keep coming around here?" he said, changing the subject.

"I'm going to marry her."

Guy looked horrified. He gaped at his father. "You can't! You can't do that! What about Mom?"

"Your mother is married," he said flatly. "I'm sure she still loves you and Amy and Polk, but she won't be coming back. You're going to have to take it like a man and learn to live with it. Life isn't a cartoon or a movie. Things don't always work out to a happy ending."

"I don't want Melody here!" Guy said harshly. "She's not going to be my mother!"

Emmett felt exasperated. Arguing was getting him nowhere. He stood up abruptly. "I'll marry whom I please," he said flatly. "If you don't like it, that's tough. But you'd better not give her any trouble," he added with quiet menace. "If her cat disappears again, or anything happens to her that upsets her, I'll hold you responsible."

Guy flushed, averting his head. The cat haunted him. He couldn't tell his father how sick he'd been when he knew Alistair might have died because of him.

"I won't bother her stupid cat," he said shortly.

Emmett sighed wearily. "The other kids love her," he said. "She's kind and gentle and if you'd give her half a chance, she'd care about you, too. But you're the original tough guy, aren't you?" his father asked. "You're Mr. Cool. Nobody is going to get close to you. Not even me."

Guy averted his eyes.

"I've done everything I can think of to reach you," Emmett continued. "Including involving you in the routine of running a ranch, but you're too busy or there's a television program on or you have to play with Barney."

"You're only doing it because she isn't around," Guy said icily. "You'd rather be with her than me."

Emmett smiled half amusedly. "When

you're a few years older, the reason will become perfectly obvious to you."

Guy flushed. "I know about girls. There's this one at school, but she thinks I'm ugly and stupid. She said so, in front of her girlfriends. I hate girls!" He stuck his hands into his jeans and glared at his father. "Especially Melody!"

Emmett could only barely remember being eleven years old and hating girls. He smiled faintly. "Well, I'm marrying her whether you like it or not," he said pleasantly.

Guy turned and stormed off into his room and slammed the door. Emmett lifted an eyebrow. Parenting, he decided, was not a job for the weakhearted. He was going to have to find some way to get to that boy, while there was still time.

The next weekend, Emmett and Melody made a formal announcement to Amy and Polk. They knew. Guy had told them already, and they were unusually reserved, glancing at their older brother uncertainly.

"Will you live with us, Melody?" Amy asked.

"Yes," Melody said quietly. "I hope we'll be good friends. I don't have a family, you know," she added without looking at them. "Only my brother."

"Yeah, her brother who stole our mother!" Guy burst out. "Well, I don't want you here...!"

"Go to your room," Emmett said. His voice was low and very quiet, but the look in his eyes made Guy obey without another word.

"Guy said you'll be mean to us," Amy told Melody worriedly. "He said you were only pretending to be nice until you hooked Emmett."

Melody went down on her knees in front of the little girl and studied the green eyes in the softly tanned thin face framed by pigtails.

"Amy, do you know how you feel with different people? I mean, you feel happy around some, and nervous and unhappy around others?"

Amy frowned. "I guess so."

"Well, sometimes when we don't know people very well, we have to trust our feelings about them. I can't promise you that I'll never be angry, that I'll never lose my temper, that I'll never hurt your feelings. I'm just a person, and I'm not perfect. But I'll love you a lot, if you'll let me," she added with a smile. "All of you. I know I'll never be your real mother, but I can be your friend and you can be mine."

Amy seemed to accept that, and to relax.

She smiled. "Polk and I think you're the greatest. Guy just doesn't want you around because he thinks Emmett and our mother will get married again someday." She grimaced. "But they won't."

Melody wondered at the wisdom in that small voice. Amy was something of a conundrum. At times she seemed much older than her eight years.

"Do you love Emmett?" Amy asked out of the blue.

Melody blushed, embarrassed.

"Yes. Do you?" Polk seconded, joining Amy, his eyes large under the spectacles as he smiled at her.

Emmett pursed his lips, and his eyes twinkled. "That's it, kids, make her tell you!"

Melody glared at him. "You can be quiet."

"I want to know," he persisted. He chuckled softly. "Never mind, then. I'll find out for myself, later."

That went right over Amy's and Polk's heads, thank goodness. They began to talk about school and soon afterward, supper was put on the table. Guy's was taken to his room by an irritable Mrs. Jenson, because he refused to come out.

The boy's behavior was the one regret in

Melody's mind when Emmett left the kids with Mrs. Jenson and drove her back to Houston.

"He isn't going to accept it," she said, when they were in her apartment and the door was closed. She looked up at Emmett worriedly. "I can't come between you and your son... Emmett!"

He'd lifted her off the floor in midspeech and carried her without a word into the dark bedroom. He laid her gently on the coverlet and slid onto it beside her. When she tried to speak, his mouth covered her protesting lips. Seconds later, she couldn't speak at all.

Guy and his attitude were forgotten in the slow, tender moments that followed. Emmett eased her out of her dress and slip so gently that she hardly noticed, and his warm mouth moved slowly over every inch of her, kindling unmanageable sensations that quickly made her writhe and moan.

Her eyes grew accustomed to the semidarkness, so that when he removed her bra, she could see his eyes glitter as he looked at her.

"Sometimes I think I dreamed you," he said huskily. Then his head bent, and what he'd once described to her began to happen all at once. His warm mouth nibbled tenderly at her taut nipples before it moved hungrily over the swollen softness around them. He held her and caressed her to the point of madness, and when his hands invaded the most intimate part of her, she was helpless, enslaved.

He whirled her body against the length of his and enveloped her while he kissed her mouth into submission. The abrasion of his jeans and shirt against her unclothed skin was as exciting as the mouth that was tutoring her own.

She clung to him when he lifted his head. He was breathing roughly and his chest was shaking with the beat of his heart. Against her stomach, she could feel the hard, impatient maleness of him.

"Emmett?" she whispered unsteadily.

"Do you want me?" he asked in a harsh, husky tone.

"Oh, yes," she said honestly.

"All of me, right now?"

"Yes!"

He sat up, and it was an effort. His hand shot out and the room exploded in light.

For a shocked instant, Melody lay on the coverlet disoriented. Then she saw him looking at her body, at the soft pink nudity that her thin white briefs did nothing to disguise, at the taut, swollen evidence of her desire. She went scarlet and began to lift her hands to her breasts to hide them.

He shook his head, and his hands caught hers. "You're mine," he said quietly. "We're engaged. That gives me the right to look at you like this. In fact, it gives me a few other rights that I'm damned tempted to exercise." His hot gaze fell to her stomach and lower, to her long, elegant legs. His hand followed his eyes, and she gasped and moved restlessly, helplessly, on the coverlet.

He eased down, his face somber, almost stern, as his fingers trespassed gently past the elastic band. He touched her and she fought him, wincing.

"Easy," he said gently. "It isn't supposed to hurt."

"It…does!"

He bent and brushed his lips tenderly against her wild eyes, her cheeks, her trembling mouth. "You're frightened. There's no need. None at all. When it happens, it will be as easy as falling into water, as easy as breathing. Your body is soft and elastic here," he whispered. "It will absorb mine, like a glove absorbing a hand."

The analogy made her shiver. He kissed her flickering eyelids, tracing her long lashes with his tongue. "I don't want you to be afraid of me. I promise that I won't hurt you, in any way."

She looked at him worriedly, her eyes big and uncertain.

He nodded. "I suppose I knew all along that it would take more than words." He reached over and turned off the lamp before he slid alongside her again. "It will be easier for you in the dark, won't it?" he whispered.

She didn't understand what he meant until it began. The soft, stroking motion kindled explosive feelings in her untried body. She tried to fight them at first, but the tide of pleasure he induced was as overwhelming as life itself. She gave in to it, gloried in it, wept and writhed and moaned in an anguish of hot, building tension that finally splintered into the most incredible surge of pleasure she'd ever imagined in her wildest dreams.

He gathered her close and held her trembling body, fighting his own demons even as he banished hers. His lips smoothed over her hot face, tenderly calming her.

"That, magnified," he whispered at her ear, "is what I'm going to give you on our wedding night."

She clung to him, dazed. "I never dreamed…!"

"You're more than I ever hoped for," he said

quietly, cradling her in his arms. "You don't tease or play games, do you? And you're not ashamed to feel what I can give you, or to admit that you do feel it."

She touched his lean cheek and felt the muscles taut in it. "I like to think I'll be able to give it back, when I know how," she murmured shyly.

He kissed her with aching tenderness. "You will," he said quietly. "Lovemaking should be mutual. I won't ever take my pleasure at your expense."

He was a surprisingly considerate man. She had a fleeting glimpse of him as a lover, and her body moved unconsciously on the coverlet.

"I want you, too, very badly," he said, feeling and understanding the movement. "But we'll wait until after we're married. I don't want a tarnished memory of our first loving. Hors d'oeuvres, on the other hand," he murmured wickedly, "are perfectly permissible."

He bent and nuzzled his mouth over her breast, feeling her instant response, hearing her urgent cry.

It couldn't last. He was too hungry for her, and the risk grew by the minute. Finally he groaned and got to his feet, shivering a little with the effort.

"I'd better go home while I still can," he mused wryly. "Don't get up. And try not to faint. I'm going to turn on the light."

She would have protested at the beginning, but it didn't matter now. He knew her almost as well as a lover.

The light came on and she lay there, letting him look at her. The briefs he'd stripped from her were tossed onto the foot of the bed. There was nothing between her and his narrow, hungry green eyes.

"I hope you don't believe in divorce," he said in a faintly strangled tone. "Because you'd have to change your name and move to the jungle to escape me."

She stretched deliberately, glorying in the growing tautness of his lean, fit body. She could imagine how it was going to feel grinding into hers, and her lips parted on a rush of breath.

"That goes double for you," she whispered. "You'll belong to me, too, when we're married."

"It's more than desire for you, isn't it?" he asked quietly.

"Yes."

He searched her eyes. "For me, too, Melody," he replied. "It's more than enough to start with. I'll arrange the ceremony for next Saturday."

"All right."

"I'll make sure I've got what we need to keep you from getting pregnant right away," he added.

"I can see the doctor and get him to put me on the pill," she began.

He sat down on the bed beside her, his eyes troubled. He drew the cover over her prone body with a rueful, reluctant smile. "Too much temptation can kill even a strong man," he said dryly. The smile faded. "Listen, I know the pill is pretty foolproof, and everybody says it's safe. But I feel uncomfortable about letting you take chances with your health."

"If I don't take the pill... Well, I've heard that some men don't like using what they have to use," she said hesitantly.

He touched her face tenderly. "Well, I'm not some men," he replied honestly. "And I believe pregnancy shouldn't be an accident."

"I know." She traced his hand where it lay on the cover beside her head. "The kids will need time, too, to get used to me before we start creating new complications."

"In the meanwhile, I can take care of it."

"If you're that worried about the pill, you

can come with me and talk to the doctor yourself," she said. "There are other ways."

"How do you feel about it?" he asked.

She flushed and averted her eyes.

He turned her face back. "It's too serious an issue to evade because of modesty. How do you feel about it?"

She searched his hard face. "I'm not afraid to take the pill. I don't think it's so risky. And I want to be…very, very close to you when we love each other," she said huskily. "As close as we can get when we fit together."

His face went ruddy. He actually shivered.

"Oh, Emmett, I want you…!" She drew him down and kissed him with helpless urgency, feeling him throw off the covers as he levered himself over her. His knee urged her legs apart and he slid between them, shaking as he pushed down, letting her feel him in total intimacy.

He groaned harshly, his body stilling suddenly as the danger of the situation cut through his desire for her.

Her body was new to pleasure and hungry for it. He understood her headlong rush toward it, but he had to protect her from a danger she still didn't understand.

"Lie still. Lord, baby, please…!"

His hands forced her a few inches away from his tormented body. She moaned, but he persisted. "Melody, it hurts me." He ground out the words.

She lay still, curious. Her big eyes found the pallor of his face even as she felt him tremble.

"Hurts?" she asked uncertainly.

He dragged her hand up against him. "Here," he said huskily. "It hurts like hell. You've got to stop moving against me. All right?"

"Yes." But she didn't move her hand, even when his withdrew. She moved back a little and looked down with open curiosity.

He saw her expression and sighed heavily. "All right. Here."

He rolled over onto his back and lay there, stoically letting her look and touch and experience him. He shivered a little, but her touch soothed more than it wounded.

She drew away almost at once, embarrassed by her own boldness, and smiled at him.

He threw the coverlet at her. She understood without words, wrapping herself up in it to remove the threat with a wicked smile on her face.

"Witch," he accused.

"You liked it," she said right back.

He stretched, winced and put his hands

under his head while he studied her. His body began to relax, but slowly.

"When you're through having anatomy lessons, I'll leave," he said pointedly.

Her eyebrows lifted. "You call this an anatomy lesson?" she asked with mock surprise. "When I'm totally nude and you're lying there with all your clothes on?"

"I'm modest," he informed her.

She pursed her lips and stared at his jeans. "Take them off. I dare you."

He laughed with pure delight. "No! Damn it, woman, have you no shame?"

"Shame is for people who don't want to have sex with other people." She leaned closer, fanning the coverlet between her breasts. "I'm famished!" she whispered with a mock leer.

He chuckled at her uninhibited display. "Come here, you torment."

He pulled her down and kissed her, but with slow, sweet tenderness, not passion. "I adore you," he whispered. "And I take it back about the jungle. If you ever want to get away from me, it had better be Mars."

"I'll keep that in mind." She kissed him back. "I really don't mind taking the pill."

He nodded. "It's your body. It has to be your

decision." He smiled ruefully. "Having just discovered you, I don't want to risk losing you."

That made her feel warm all over. "You won't," she said softly. She pushed back his thick, dark hair. "Can I love you?"

He threw his arms out to either side and closed his eyes. "Go ahead."

She hit him. "You know what I mean."

He searched her face for a long moment. "You're serious."

"Yes." She traced his chin and then his mouth as her eyes levered back up to hold his.

He smoothed his hands over her shoulders, under the coverlet, savoring her magnolia-petal skin. "Love is important to a woman, isn't it?" he asked with faint cynicism.

"It's important to most men, too," she said softly. Her eyes were warm and steady, without deceit. "I'm going to love you anyway. I just thought it would be polite to ask. But if you're going to be difficult about it, just pretend you don't notice that I'm crazy about you."

He sighed and smiled. "It would be pretty difficult to miss. Even your breasts blush when I look at you."

"They do not... Emmett!"

She made a grab for the cover, but it was too late. "See?" he asked, nodding toward the faint ruddy color below her collarbone. But the smile faded almost at once. He touched her reverently. "You are so incredibly lovely," he whispered, almost choking on the emotion he felt. He closed his eyes and dragged himself off the bed. "I have to go. Now. Immediately. Without delay."

She had to fight back a smile at his desperate look. She pulled the cover back around her and got up, looking so smug that he glowered at her.

"Proud of yourself?" he muttered, blatantly aroused and with no way to hide it from the new wisdom in her twinkling brown eyes.

She glanced down and back up. "Yep," she said, grinning.

He laughed defeatedly, shaking his head. "I'm out of here."

"Until Saturday," she reminded him pertly as she walked with him to the door. "After that, you're mine!"

"And you're mine," he returned. He caught the doorknob and glanced down at her with quiet introspection, taking in her flushed face, her swollen mouth, her joy-filled eyes. His soul seemed to clench at the pleasure it gave him to want her.

She saw that tension and understood it. "I

won't ever hurt you," she said suddenly, dead serious. "But I'll love you until it hurts. If you really don't want that, you'd better say so now. Once I've lived with you, I honestly don't know if I can let go…"

He pressed his fingers against her lips. "You won't have to," he said quietly. "Love doesn't come with money-back guarantees. It's a risk. We'll take it together."

"All right."

He sighed gently, and he smiled at her. "Sleep well."

"No, I won't," she said.

"Neither will I." His eyes darkened. "I do want you so desperately," he said huskily, emotion throbbing in his voice.

"Then stay with me," she invited quietly.

"I want to," he said fervently. "But we'll do things properly. Not for our sakes, but for the children's. A white wedding may be old-fashioned in this unstructured society, but I want one for us."

She smiled at him. "So do I. But I'd do anything for you."

Incredible, the burst of inner light he felt at the words. He smiled, a little dazedly as he let it ripple through him. "Anything?" he murmured.

She studied him. "Well, almost anything. I wouldn't kiss a snake or eat a chocolate-covered ant for you."

He bent and kissed her quickly. "Okay. No kissing snakes and eating ants. Now good night!"

"Good night."

He winked at her and went out the door. She locked it behind him. On second thought, she mused privately, if it wasn't a venomous snake, and she could keep her eyes closed while she kissed it...

Emmett had just finished arranging the small service when Guy came into his office, his hands in his back pockets, looking repentant but still belligerent.

"Well?" Emmett asked curtly.

Guy's thin shoulders rose and fell. "I'm sorry," he said stiffly.

"For what?"

"What I said. The way I acted." Guy stared at the floor. "My mom really won't come back?"

"No."

He took a slow, audible breath before he glanced at his father. "But she didn't go away because of me?"

"Of course not," Emmett said. "She loves all you kids. If you want to know, I wouldn't let her near you after she left," he confessed heavily. "I was wrong, too. Dead wrong. If you want to see her, talk to her, it's all right."

Guy didn't say anything for a minute. "Melody hates me, doesn't she?"

"No. It isn't in her nature to hate people," Emmett said quietly. "But you haven't gone out of your way to endear yourself to her, either."

"Yeah. She won't forget about the cat, I guess."

"If you meet her halfway, it won't matter at all," Emmett said. "You have to compromise. I'm a hell of a bad teacher, in that respect, but I'm learning. We'll both have to learn."

"Okay. I'll try."

Emmett smiled. "And you might reconsider getting used to the business side of ranch work," he added.

Guy shrugged. "I guess I could." He glanced warily at his father. Emmett looked pretty different lately. He looked happy.

"Things going better at school, are they?"

"Since I beat up Buddy Haskell, they're going great," Guy said simply.

"You what?"

"He made a remark about smelly ranchers

who walk around all day in cow...well, in ma-
nure." Guy corrected himself, grinning. "He
said you smelled like that, so I pasted him one.
The teacher was too busy talking to the other
teachers to even notice." He chuckled. "He told
her he walked into a door."

Emmett looked skyward. "Now, listen,
here..."

"Homework to do," Guy said quickly. "Have
to get on it, right now. I'm helping Polk with
fractions." He frowned. "Isn't it amazing that
he can do multiplication in his head but he
can't add a fourth and a half?"

"He'll be a rocket scientist one day," Emmett replied.

"God help us if he can't do fractions by
then," Guy mused. He left his father sitting
there and went to get his books.

Emmett felt a glimmer of hope that Guy
would change his attitude. If Guy came around,
it would be clear sailing for sure. Except that
Adell was pregnant, and he should have told
the boy. Well, there was no need, and plenty of
time for him to find it out. Plenty of time, now.

Chapter 9

The wedding was held at the local Methodist church. Ted Regan came down for it, and so did Tansy, Logan and Kit Deverell. Amy was flower girl and Polk carried the rings on a pillow. Guy sat stiffly on the pew reserved for family, having declined belligerently any sort of participation in the wedding.

Despite the talk he'd had with his father, he'd still hoped that his mother might come along at the last minute and stop the service, say that she was wrong, that she loved his father and wanted to marry him again. But it didn't happen. Nobody wanted him, he thought suddenly. His mother had run away and never even phoned or written, and now his dad wanted somebody's company besides his. He glanced at his brother and sister, so radiant at the thought of their new stepmother. He'd have to make the most of it. He was sorry that he'd made things so hard for Melody. He hoped that his dad was right, and she didn't have a vengeful nature.

As he watched, Emmett spoke the words, put the ring on Melody's finger and lifted her short veil. He looked at her for a long, long time before he finally bent and kissed her. It was the gentlest kiss she'd ever had from him, one of respect and affection and delight. She gave it back in the same way, brimming with joy.

After the service, Ted Regan stopped long enough to congratulate them. Having heard him called "old man Regan," Melody's first glimpse of him was a surprise. He wasn't old, but he did have prematurely silver hair, a great shock of it, combed to one side. He had pale blue eyes and a long, lean, very tanned face. He reminded her of the actor, Randolph Scott, an impression that was emphasized when he spoke in a slow Texas drawl.

"Can't say I've ever wanted to marry any-body," Ted mused, "but I guess it's all right for some people. Best of luck. Don't even think about going back to San Antonio," he added as he shook Emmett's hand and his blue eyes glittered like cold steel. "I'll hunt you down and drag you back here at the end of a rope if you even try. You've accomplished more in a month than any other foreman I've hired accomplished in a year. I'll even give you a half interest in the place if that's what it takes to keep you."

Emmett felt a foot taller. Marrying Melody was delight enough, but praise from tight-lipped Ted Regan was something of a rarity and accepted with pride.

"Thanks," Emmett told the other man, who was as tall and fit as he was himself, despite the fact that Ted was almost forty years old. "I like my job a lot. I can't think of anything that would make me quit at the moment." He frowned. "Maybe if a cow fell in the well…"

"I don't think you could stuff a calf down that wellhead," Ted reminded him. "Unless it was cooked and ground up."

"Point taken. I'll stay for a spell."

"Good." He clamped his white Stetson back on his head and tilted it at a rakish angle. "I'm off to Colorado for the national cattlemen's meeting. More damned politics than horses in the industry these days." He walked off, shaking his head.

"He's never married? Really?" Melody asked her new husband as she watched the tall man walk away.

"They say there isn't a woman in south Texas brave enough," Emmett said under his breath. "He's very pleasant in company, but he can scorch leather when he's upset. We've got two old cowboys who hide in the barn every time he stops by to check the books!"

"You don't," she implored.

He chuckled, drawing her against his side as they moved lazily toward the car where the kids were waiting. "Oh, Ted and I get along pretty well. Peas in a pod, you know." He glanced at her mischievously. "Or didn't you know that I can scorch leather, too, on occasion?"

She leaned closer. "I'll settle for having you scorch me tonight," she whispered.

He drew in a breath. "Lady, that kind of talk will get you ravished on the hood of the car," he said with an uncomfortable look. "Shame on you, saying such things to a man, and near a church, too!"

"No better place for it," she said gently. "We're married. With my body, I thee worship…?" She wiggled her hand with the plain gold band she'd asked for on her third finger under his nose.

"Shameless," he repeated.

"Yes. And tonight you'll be on your knees giving thanks that I am," she said smugly.

He glanced at her. "You'll be the one on your knees, begging for mercy."

She grinned at him. "Promise?" She wiggled her eyebrows.

He laughed out loud and hugged her. Probably she was bluffing, but he didn't mind at all. He'd never been so happy in all his life. Except for Guy's attitude, he amended, watching the boy's faintly reticent stare as they approached him.

Guy's face set in familiar lines, unsmiling and resentful, and Emmett lost his temper at that look, not realizing that Guy was nervous and intimidated because he wanted to congratulate them but was uncertain of the reaction he was going to get from Melody.

Emmett wasn't about to let the boy put a damper on Melody's wedding day. Best way to avoid trouble was with a good strong offensive, he thought. "Put a sock in it," he told Guy when he opened his mouth to speak. "Or you can go and pay a visit to that military school we've talked about."

Melody was shocked at the threat and the expression it produced on Guy's face.

She started to protest, but Emmett stopped her.

"I've given you more rope than you've earned," he told Guy coldly. "I won't plead with you anymore. Melody is my wife. If you can't accept that, a good private school is the best answer. I enjoyed it. You might, too."

Guy's pallor was obvious. He swallowed. "I don't want to go away to school," he said heavily.

"That's your only other option," Emmett said.

Guy's head lifted with what pride he could manage. "I'm ready to go home when you are." He glanced at Melody and away. "Congratulations," he said in a ghostly tone, and turned to get into the backseat with an excited Amy and Polk.

Melody's heart ached for his wounded pride. "Oh, Emmett…!" she moaned.

He averted his gaze from her pleading eyes. "Some boys take a firm hand," he said curtly. "I've been too lenient with all three of them, and they've gone wild. It's never pleasant to

get the upper hand back once you've lost it."
He looked at her. "I won't hurt the boy. I won't
send him away unless I have to. But you must
see that allowing him to persecute you and
dictate to me is impossible. He's only eleven
years old."

"I know. But…"

He bent and kissed her gently. "It will take
time. We both knew that from the beginning.
Stop trying to gulp down the future. We
haven't begun."

"All right. I'll try."

She wasn't going to give up, though. She'd
wait until he was less tense and then approach
him about Guy. She really couldn't let him
send the boy away before she'd even tried to
make friends with him. It was Guy's home as
well as Emmett's and hers. The look on the
boy's face haunted her.

They took the kids home and a beaming
Mrs. Jenson congratulated them while Melody
changed into a simple gray dress for travel.
They were going to have a three-day honeymoon down in Cancún. The kids were bitterly
disappointed that they couldn't go, but Melody promised Amy and Polk that they'd go as
a family very soon. Amy had remarked that
she guessed newly married people did need a

little time alone. A remark that sent Emmett into gales of laughter.

Guy didn't speak to his father. Melody stopped just in front of him as Emmett was saying goodbye to the other kids.

"He won't do it" was all she said. She smiled. "It will be all right, you know."

Guy was shocked. He couldn't even speak. He hadn't expected her to say anything to him after the way he'd treated her. Now he needed to talk, and he couldn't.

It was too late, anyway. She was gone, with his father.

"They look nice together, don't you think?" Amy asked with a sigh. She glared at Guy. "You're going to get it when Emmett gets back. You were awful at their wedding."

"I'm not going to get it, but you are if you don't watch your mouth," Guy said, daring her.

"Will you two stop fighting? Look, Alistair likes to play with a string!" Polk called, dangling a string while the cat played with it.

The big tabby was staying at the ranch, and Mrs. Jenson had ironclad orders not to let him out. Guy went to stand by Polk and Amy while he watched the cat. He hoped Alistair had a forgiving nature, as well as Melody, or things could get real hectic here.

* * *

Cancún was a vision. The colors of the sea and the blistering white of the beach, the modern Mexican architecture with exaggerated Mayan motifs made a potpourri of images that Melody found fascinating. She'd been to Mexico before, but never to this particular part of it. Despite the crowd of tourists, she drank in the atmosphere with delight.

Emmett looked good in white swimming trunks. She admired his long, tanned legs with covetous eyes, not to mention his broad, hair-matted chest and arms and flat stomach. He was delicious, and a lot of other women seemed to think so, because they kept walking by with their flabby, white-skinned husbands, staring unashamedly at him.

"One more time, lady, and I'm going to leap up and crown you with my tanning lotion," Melody muttered under her breath.

"What was that?" Emmett asked without opening his eyes.

"That skinny brunette. She keeps walking by, leering at you."

"My, my, are you jealous?" he teased.

She stared at him without blinking. "Why don't you go back to the room with me and find out?"

His heart began to beat wildly. "We've only been here an hour or so. I thought you might be too tired," he said gently.

She shook her head very slowly. Her long hair was loosened, blowing softly in the ocean breeze. She searched his green eyes. "I want you," she whispered.

His body reacted sharply and he laughed with self-conscious delight. "Damn it, woman…!"

"Recite multiplication tables," she whispered with a gleeful smile.

He glared at her. "You'd better have packed something that prevents multiplication, because I forgot to."

"I did." She'd decided on the pill, despite his objections, because she felt it was the safest way to prevent a child until they were ready. She stood up, holding out her hand. "I've waited twenty years," she murmured dryly. "I do hope you're going to be worth it."

He got to his feet, his pale eyes shimmering with a kind of knowledge that made her blush. "Honey, I can guarantee it."

He took her hand and they went back to the room in a tense, delicious silence.

She went straight into his arms the minute the door closed, determined not to admit that she was nervous of him this way. It was broad daylight, but waiting until tonight would have inhibited both of them. Besides, she thought as she lifted her face to look at him, she loved him. It would be all right, as long as he didn't compare her with any of his past lovers. She hoped that she was going to be enough for him, because despite her bravado, she felt vaguely inadequate.

But that fear was quickly forgotten when he bent to kiss her, and the heat of his body and the skill of his mouth and hands turned her nervous response into sensual fever.

He eased her onto the bed and very efficiently moved everything out of his way, so that her nude body was cradled to his in the slow preliminary to their first loving.

"Shh," he whispered when she began to writhe and pull at him. "Not so fast, little one. Don't gulp it. Sip it. Slow down."

"It aches," she whispered unsteadily as his mouth teased and tormented hers. "I ache all over."

"So do I," he said on soft, unsteady laughter. "But we're building to one hell of an explosion, and it's too soon for you, despite what you think. No, don't touch me like that, not yet," he said softly, stilling her hand. "This is all for you. My turn will come later, when I've satisfied you to the tips of your pretty pink toes. Kiss me, sweetheart."

He coaxed her mouth back up to his and his hands moved again, tasting her body as his mouth tasted her lips, and then settled hungrily on her breasts and her soft, flat stomach, experiencing, exploring her, making her crazy for his possession.

"I can't...bear it...!" she whimpered finally, anguish in her wide, haunted eyes. "Oh, please...!"

"All right," he whispered tenderly, moving over her. "Gently, little one," he breathed. "Gently, gently."

He held her firmly, his face above hers, his muscular body cording as he positioned her and began to move down. He was afraid of hurting her, even as it excited him beyond bearing to be her first lover. But she didn't flinch, didn't fight. She lay there, shivering, her eyes open and fixed with pain and wonder on his taut face as he invaded the sweet, warm softness of her innocence and was slowly, painstakingly engulfed by it.

She flinched and he grimaced, stilling until she relaxed again. He could barely breathe. "Is it bad?" he managed to ask.

"It was. It's not now." She closed her eyes and willed her body to accept him. And it did, abruptly, and generously. She let out a long sigh of relief.

He moved as close as he could then, fighting a hellish surge of tense pleasure that begged for relief.

"It doesn't hurt anymore," she whispered shyly. Imagine, talking to a man while you were doing this!

"That's what you think," he groaned.

"Oh, Emmett," she breathed. She lifted to him, watching him shiver. She liked his reaction. She felt suddenly confident, all woman. She lifted again. He protested, but he didn't try to stop her. His face clenched and he breathed roughly. She loved him. It was going to be so beautiful.

"Witch!" he groaned.

"Do you like it?" she teased, moving sensually.

"I'll show you how much I like it," he breathed with a smiling threat. He whipped over onto his side, taking her with him. His strong, lean hands caught her hips and he laughed with something savage, untamed, in his pale eyes as he slid one long leg between both of hers and began to rock her in that deep intimacy.

She gasped as pleasure began to sting her body with bursts of throbbing heat.

"Did you think you could match me so quickly?" he whispered with passionate tenderness as he teased her mouth with his. And all the while, his hands pulled and pushed and teased while he invaded her trembling innocence. He watched her face the whole time, enjoying the stunned wonder of her dark eyes. "How does this feel?" he whispered.

She cried out at the shock of pleasure that came with the movement. Her hands caught at his powerful arms, but the great waves of sensation kept coming, faster and faster, his whole body an instrument of pleasure as he held her and quickly deepened his possession, laughing like a devil as he drove her down into the fires of fulfillment and watched her body splinter into ecstasy against the hard whip of his passion.

Only when she began to cry out in a hoarse, sobbing oblivion did he allow himself the delight of joining her in that lofty plane of mindless joy.

The explosions of pleasure surged through him like tidal waves, lifting, slamming into him, burning him in feverish delight. He called her name, again and again, clutching her to him as he gave in to satiation.

It wasn't like other times, other women. He shivered, but he couldn't stop. His lean hands pulled her into him, over him, and he moved helplessly under her soft, warm body, coaxing her mouth down to cover his as he began the rhythm all over again.

She hadn't imagined what it would be like. He was inexhaustible, incoherent in his passion, but the skill and mastery were beyond her dreams. He raised her to levels she couldn't have pictured, gave her endless ecstasy, made her alternately wanton and exhausted as the day turned finally to night.

When she was too tired to turn her head to kiss him, she fell into a deep, dreamless sleep.

A sweet smell and the feel of light disturbed her. Light shone into her eyes. She put up a hand and felt the warmth of sunlight filtering in through the venetian blinds.

She opened her eyes. Emmett was holding a warm pastry under her nose, letting her smell it.

"Hungry?" he asked softly, smiling at her.

He was fully dressed and she was wearing a sheer blue nightgown. She didn't remember putting it on, but she must have. She smiled back at him. "Starved. Oh!"

She moved and grimaced. He chuckled wickedly, because he knew why she'd grimaced.

"Are you sore?" he asked with mock sympathy.

"Yes, I'm sore," she murmured, blushing. "I hope your back is broken…"

He kissed her gently, stemming the words. "You're the best lover I've ever had," he whispered.

"But I couldn't be," she protested. "I didn't know anything."

"Yes, you did," he replied, kissing her eyelids shut. "You knew how to love me, and you did. It was the most beautiful, the most exquisitely fulfilling night of my life. Even Mars won't be far enough for you to run to get away from me now. I've just been farther out than that in your arms."

She sighed and snuggled closer to him. "Now I know what they meant, when they said it was like eating potato chips." She laughed delightedly. "Oh, Emmett, I like it!"

"I'm glad. So do I." He lifted his head and cocked a rueful eyebrow. "I suppose for a few days now we'll be good friends and companions."

She peered at him through her long lashes. "In health class, nobody ever said you got sore."

"That was my fault," he said, and looked guilty. "I should have stopped after the first time. I'm sorry. It had been a long time and you went to my head. But I should have had more control."

"I wasn't complaining," she said sincerely. "I loved it. I'd do it all over again if I could."

"So would I. That's the hell of it." He brushed his mouth gently against hers. "Was it worth the wait?" he asked seriously, searching her soft, dark eyes.

"Yes," she whispered. "It was worth waiting all my life for."

"For me, too," he replied tersely. "My God, I never dreamed it would feel like that with you." He touched her face gently. "Mrs. Deverell," he said as he kissed her forehead with aching tenderness. "Mrs. Melody Deverell."

She looped her arms around his neck and nuzzled her face into his warm throat. "I'm still sleepy."

Her vulnerability made him strong, made him ache with tenderness. He bent and lifted her, carrying her to the armchair. He sat down with her in his lap and put down the pastry. Then he lifted a cup of hot coffee to her lips.

She sipped it, staring at him curiously.

"What do you want to do today?" he asked quietly.

"Stay with you."

He smiled. "What else?"

"Nothing," she said. "Only that." She reached up and put her lips gently to his. "I love you so much. More than anything or anyone in all the world." She kissed him again and felt him tremble.

He put the coffee cup down and turned her against his broad, bare chest. He held her gently, undemanding, for a long time, staring across her bright head to the window. "Go to sleep," he breathed at her temple. "I'll hold you while you sleep."

She smiled drowsily and curled closer to him, resting her cheek on his shoulder.

She slept and he watched her, fascinated by the color in her face, the soft sigh of her breath against his throat, the trusting, tender posture of her body in his arms. He thought that he'd never been so happy in all his life.

But with that feeling came a quiet regret that their first intimacy had been so turbulent.

She'd given in to him, loved him, responded completely to his fierce ardor. He should have given her tenderness instead of raw passion. It was just that it had been so long and he'd wanted her so desperately. He couldn't hold back.

Now, looking down at her sleeping face, he felt an aching need to cradle her against him in bed and show her the most exquisite kind of tenderness.

Next time, he promised himself. The thing was, she wouldn't be capable of intimacy for several days; probably not until they went home again. He grimaced. Well. Better late than never. After a minute, he closed his eyes and fell asleep himself, wrapped in her warmth and love.

When Melody and Emmett drove up at the front door of the ranch house, Guy was peering out the window. He'd worried himself sick about how he was going to keep Emmett from shipping him off to a military school. He didn't know how he was going to cope with so many changes at once. He was no longer part of his own family. Now he was going to be an outsider in Emmett and Melody's, an unwanted burden. Amy and Polk were ecstatic.

They would accept Melody and love her and be loved by her. He wasn't sure that he could fit in. She might still be pretending to care about him, until she was settled with his father. Some of his friends at school had stepparents. He'd heard some terrible stories about that. Oh, why, why, did people have to get divorced? he agonized.

Melody had hugged Amy and Polk and greeted Mrs. Jenson. She came into the house, looking for Guy. He glanced at her warily.

"How are you?" she asked.

He shrugged, painfully shy. She looked radiant. It was a contrast of some magnitude to the way he looked, and felt.

"Guy. You might at least say hello," Emmett said, interfering all too quickly, his green eyes flashing.

"Hello," Guy replied, dropping his eyes.

Melody put her fingers against Emmett's hard mouth. "Let's get our clothes changed. I want to pass out the presents," she said, before Emmett could do any more damage to her fragile relationship with Guy. "I brought stuff for all of you," she told the children. "Even Mrs. Jenson."

"Why, how sweet of you, Mrs. Deverell!" the older woman exclaimed. She hadn't anticipated liking Emmett's young wife. But the woman was not what she expected. She beamed. "I'll just fix some coffee and cake."

She went off toward the kitchen with an excited Amy and Polk, while Guy sat down on the sofa, idly stroking Alistair. The cat seemed to like him. It was forever following him around and purring. He was glad something liked him. Even Amy and Polk had been resentful and unkind since the wedding. He felt alone in the world except for this cat he'd been so cruel to in the beginning.

"I'm glad you like me, Alistair," he told the tabby.

Alistair looked up with half-closed green eyes and purred even louder.

"You can't be cruel to him," Melody told Emmett gently when they were cloistered in the master bedroom. "He'll try. I know he will, and so will I. You can't expect him to be instantly happy, Emmett. It's hard for him. Really hard."

He sighed heavily, drawing her gently to him. "I'm impatient. Too impatient sometimes." He searched her soft eyes and something alien flared in his as he touched her face. "I can't bear the thought of letting anything or anyone hurt you," he said hesitantly. He drew her close, feeling her soft response to the words as he bent to kiss her. "I can't bear to let you out of my sight…"

She kissed him back, hungry for him because even though they'd been passionate lovers that one time, they hadn't been able to make love again because it had taken such a long time for her to recover from his ardor that first day.

His tall, powerful body began to vibrate, to harden. "I want you," he choked, and his mouth became insistent.

"Tonight," she promised, smiling at him. "Oh, Emmett, tonight…!"

When they rejoined the family, several hectic minutes later, Melody was flushed and shy and Emmett was grinding his teeth. But he looked at her with wonder and delight. It got better and better, he thought. The walls were thick, but she was still a little shy. He'd have to have a radio on or something tonight. Tonight. His body began to throb and he went off into the kitchen to see about coffee.

Melody passed out presents: a set of Mexican coins and a cup and string-tied ball toy for Amy; a book on the Mayans and a few replicated artifacts for Polk, who seemed bent on being an archaeologist. And for Guy, a serape and a pocketknife with a hand-carved handle.

Guy was speechless. He'd wanted a pocketknife of his own for ages, because he loved to whittle things out of wood. He was forever borrowing his father's. Melody had noticed. Imagine that, he thought regretfully. He'd been terrible to her, but she'd gone to a lot of trouble to buy something he really wanted.

He looked up at her, shyly.

"Do you like it?" she asked, frowning. "I wasn't sure…"

"It's great!" he said slowly. "Thanks."

"Don't abuse the privilege," Emmett told him firmly. "You can't use it to carve your initials in the walls or make devices of torture to use on unsuspecting tourists."

Guy grinned. "Sure, Dad."

It was the first time he'd seen the boy smile in weeks. He glanced at Melody and nodded. She'd known, and he hadn't, the way to his son's heart. He had a lot to learn about his own children and his new wife.

Amy tugged at his sleeve. "Emmett, it was very nice of you to think of us on your honeymoon," she said, smiling radiantly at him.

"It sure was!" Polk enthused. "Look at this

atl-atl," he said, displaying the use of the Aztec throwing stick that looked something like an arrow on a slab of bamboo. "Ancient Aztecs used to hunt with these, did you know?"

"I know about dinosaurs and Pleistocene animals," Emmett corrected him. "My minor was paleontology, not archaeology."

"Archaeology is a branch of anthropology," Polk said authoritatively. "I'm going to study it when I get out of high school. Just think, Dad, maybe I'll be the one to find the first Homo erectus remains in the United States!"

Emmett frowned. "There's no proof that Homo erectus ever set foot here."

"Yet," Polk said. And grinned.

Amy tugged on Emmett's sleeve again. "Emmett?"

"Hmm?" he murmured, still distracted by Polk's question.

"Are you and Melody going to have any babies?"

Emmett stared at her. "What?"

"Babies. You know. People have sex and they get babies." She grinned. "I learned about that on television. There was this movie and it showed what people do in bed together." She frowned. "Do you and Melody have sex?"

Melody went scarlet and Emmett actually blushed.

"Shut up, Amy!" Guy muttered. "Honest to God, are you ever going to grow up? Come on, let's go outside and play with Polk's atl-atl."

"It's mine! I didn't say you could play with it!" Polk raged, his glasses sparkling.

"I'll let you see my knife," Guy offered.

The smaller boy hesitated. "Well…"

Guy put an arm around Polk and led him toward the door. "Just think, Polk, I can whittle arrows for that atl-atl. If we set up a fort just down past the barn, we can lie in wait for that nasty-tempered old bull…"

"You shoot one arrow at that bull and I'll stop your allowance forever!" Emmett called after them.

"Aw, Dad!" Guy groaned.

"I mean it!"

Amy went with the boys, glowering at her father. "Emmett, you're not the same man since we moved down here. You never let us have fun anymore."

"Considering what you people call fun, it's a miracle I haven't had to bail all three of you out of jail!"

Amy just shook her head and went out behind the boys.

"See?" Melody told him. "Guy will come around. It will take time, that's all. He's already loosening up, didn't you notice?"

He had. Guy was much more like his old self, like the boy he'd been before Emmett ever saw Melody in Logan's office. He drew her close and kissed her softly. "All right. I give in." He eased her across his lap on the sofa and kissed her more thoroughly, feeling the warmth and tenderness of it right through his body.

"I love you," she whispered, smiling against his mouth.

"Kiss me...!"

He gathered her up and devoured her until they were both trembling. His mouth slid down to her throat and he held her, shivering. He was afraid. He'd never been so afraid. She possessed him, delighted him, made him whole. He'd lost his father, whom he idolized. His mother had killed herself. Adell had left him. If he lost Melody...!

"Emmett!" she protested gently, because his arms were bruising her.

He lifted his dark head and looked at her. The expression on his face, in his eyes, touched her deeply.

She reached up to press soft, tender kisses

against his fearful eyes, his cheeks, his nose, his mouth until she felt him begin to relax. Then she drew back and searched his eyes.

"Emmett, I will never leave you," she whispered, and put her fingers over his mouth when he tried to speak. "Never," she repeated, understanding what was bothering him. She put her mouth against his and held on, feeling him shiver as he gathered her against him and kissed her with quiet desperation.

She knew then that he felt something powerful for her, even if he'd never said so. She smoothed his hair and lay quietly in his arms until the brunt of his passion was spent. Then she curled against him, trustingly, and sighed.

He stared over her head toward the door, a little less horrified than he'd been. How shocking, he thought, to discover so late in life that he'd never known what love was. At least, not until now.

Chapter 10

Emmett wanted to tell Melody what he felt. He wanted to shout it to the world. But he couldn't manage it. He felt choked up with the knowledge. He looked down at her and his heart seemed to swell to the point of bursting.

"You delight me," he whispered huskily. His hand touched her hair, her cheek. "Oh, God, I'd do anything for you…!"

She drew his mouth down to hers again and kissed him tenderly.

"Coffee's on," Mrs. Jenson said with a wicked smile as she came into the room with a tray. "I suppose you newlyweds would rather live on kisses than cake, but here it is, anyway. If you need anything else, just call."

"Thanks, Mrs. Jenson," Emmett murmured.

Melody shyly climbed off Emmett's lap to sit beside him on the sofa. "Yes, indeed, it looks delicious!" she said enthusiastically.

"Could you peek out the window occasionally?" Emmett called to Mrs. Jenson. "Just to make sure the kids aren't making shish kebab of any of old man Regan's cattle?"

"Why do you think the curtains aren't drawn?" she asked, tongue-in-cheek. "All the same, they're a nice bunch of kids. They went down to Mark Gary's cabin yesterday with a straggly bunch of old silk flowers they found. His dog got run over in the road and they felt sorry for him. Guy even offered to give him Barney because he was so upset."

Emmett was touched. He didn't seem to know his own kids at all. "That was nice of them."

"Yes, it was. They've got a lot of heart." She twisted her apron. "Of course, there was this one little incident while you were away."

"Little?" he asked hesitantly.

She shifted. "Well, you know how they feel about that inspector who comes out here—the one who yelled at Barney and made Amy cry? The one everybody in the county hates?"

Emmett's face hardened. "I had words with him about upsetting Amy."

"You weren't here," she pointed out. "He made a remark that Guy didn't like about that big Appaloosa stallion of yours that Guy adores. Then he made a couple of remarks about you."

"What did they do?" Emmett asked with resignation.

"Nothing really vicious…"

"What did they do?" he repeated.

She grimaced. "They put a potato in his tailpipe."

"Did he take it out?"

She cleared her throat. "He was too busy at the time."

"Doing what?"

"Trying to get the snake out of his front seat."

Emmett buried his face in his hands. "Oh, my God!" he wailed. "He'll shut us down for sure!"

"I don't think so."

There was hope? He lifted his head. "Why?"

"Well, the kids had some food coloring they got out of the cabinet. They sort of colored the snake up before they put it in the cab. I don't like snakes, you know, but it was real pretty. Sort of blue and pink and yellow and green, with polka dots." She shrugged. "It seems that the gentleman went back to his office and told them he'd been shut up in his car with a blue and pink and yellow and green polka-dotted snake by three midget commandos." She wiped her hands on her apron. "I hear he's having therapy. There's this new inspector. He's real nice, and he likes snakes. We, uh, didn't let him see Guy's, of course. The food coloring will wear off, eventually."

Emmett hadn't stopped laughing when she got back to the kitchen.

Melody could hardly contain herself. She hoped that the kids never got it in for her!

Guy was nervous around his father. He hadn't forgotten the threat about military school, and there was the incident with the snake. He was sure Mrs. Jenson had mentioned it.

Because he was uncertain of his position now that Melody was in residence, he tried to keep out of everyone's way.

That night, an impatient Emmett hustled the

kids to bed and turned off the television long before the news was due to come on.

He held out his hand, his eyes quiet and tender as they met Melody's.

"You look impatient, Mr. Deverell," she said demurely as he tugged her along the hall toward their bedroom.

"Impatient, desperate and a few other things. How I wish these walls were soundproof," he muttered under his breath. He closed the door and locked it before he turned on the radio by the bed to a country-western station. He looked down at Melody, who was blushing. He drew her against him and bent to brush his mouth sensuously over her own. "We're starving for each other," he whispered. "I don't want eavesdroppers, and we both get pretty vocal when we let go in bed."

"Yes." She shivered as his hands smoothed down her body. "It's been so long—!" Her voice broke.

"Eons." He lifted her onto the bed and followed her down.

Tenderness still wasn't possible, he thought as the room began to spin around them. Not yet…!

Later, when the anguish of wanting each other was spent, he aroused her again, but tenderly this time. He moved against her in a soft, sweet rhythm that was unlike anything they'd ever done together. All the while, he looked into her eyes and smoothed away her damp hair, kissed her forehead, her nose, her cheeks, her eyes. Until speech was no longer possible, he whispered broken endearments and praise.

When the spiral caught them, her body convulsed violently, despite the slow, gentle rhythm, and she began to sob under the warm crush of his mouth. The rainbow of sensation made her cry out and he was vaguely aware of the radio drowning out the sound as his muscles corded and his hips arched violently, convulsively, against her.

They were both shaking with reaction when the room came back into focus. She was crying softly, because the force of the ecstasy he'd given her had been devastating.

"I wanted to give you tenderness," he whispered with exhausted regret. "I wanted it to be soft and slow and gentle and I couldn't...!"

"But it was," she protested. She lifted up, resting her arm across his damp, throbbing chest as she looked down into his eyes. "Emmett, it was!"

"Not at the last," he said through his teeth.

"Oh. Then. Well, of course not," she murmured shyly. She smiled at him wickedly and laughed deep in her throat. "You lose control," she whispered. "I like to watch you cry out, and know that it's because of me, because of the pleasure you get from my body."

He touched her face with wonder. "I like to watch you for the same reason. Melody," he said quietly, "I never watched before. The pleasure I gave never mattered that much before."

"I'm glad." She drew her face gently against his, wrapping him up in the sweetness of her adoration. "I'd die for you, Emmett," she whispered.

He drew her down and enveloped her hungrily. His hands in her hair were unsteady as he used them to turn her head so that he could find her mouth. His lips trembled, too, with the rage of feeling she unleashed in him.

Incredible man, she thought dizzily. So much a man...

She eased her hips over his and coaxed his body into deep intimacy, pressing soft kisses over his hair-roughened chest as she shifted over him until he groaned. He lay like a pagan sacrifice, and she sat up, feeling the power of her own femininity as he writhed and moaned beneath the slow movement of her hips.

"I love you," she whispered, increasing the pressure. "I love you, Emmett, I love you!"

His lean hands bit into her hips and he arched, crying out helplessly as she fulfilled him and, in the process, herself. In the back of her mind she was grateful for the radio. If those kids had heard... She moved again and he lost the ability to think at all.

Breakfast was uncomfortable for the whole next week.

"You sure must like country-western music a lot, Emmett," Amy muttered. "But does it have to be so loud?"

"All those wailing cowboys," Polk said with a shake of his unruly hair.

"Sounds more like rock music than country," Amy agreed.

Melody's face was scarlet. She didn't dare look at Emmett. The muffled laughter coming from the head of the table was bad enough.

"I'll try to keep the volume down," Emmett promised dryly. "It helps us sleep."

"That's right," Melody agreed.

"Bill Turner wants me to go hunting with him Saturday," Guy remarked. "We're going after squirrels."

"No," Melody said abruptly.

Guy glared at her. "I can go if I want to."

"No," she said flatly. "Emmett?"

He glanced at her and frowned. She was giving him muted signals that he didn't understand. But if she was that vehement about it, there had to be a reason.

"Dad?" Guy asked belligerently.

"Melody said no," Emmett replied. "Eat your eggs."

"She's not my mother!" Guy burst out. "She can't tell me what to do!"

"She's my wife, and the hell she can't tell you what to do! This is her house now, just as much as it's mine and Amy's and Polk's and yours!"

Guy got up from the table. "I hate her!" he raged. He turned and ran out of the house. He'd wanted to go hunting more than anything in the world. It would have been the first time he'd ever shot a rifle, ever hunted anything. He'd been sure Emmett would let him go, and now that interfering woman was telling him he couldn't and Emmett took her side against his! He hated her! He ran off into the small wooded glade past the barn and stayed there for the rest of the afternoon, refusing to budge even when Amy and Polk came to find him.

"Why didn't you want him to go?" Emmett

asked Melody after Guy and the other two had gone. "Is it the thought of shooting a squirrel that bothers you?"

"It's the thought of Bill shooting him," she replied worriedly. "Emmett, the weekend before we married, Bill was out beyond the barn with a .22 rifle shooting wildly all around the place. He wasn't even aiming at anything. I yelled at him when one of the bullets whizzed past me and he stopped."

"Why didn't you tell me?" he demanded.

"He begged me not to. He said you might fire him." She looked up at him. "He promised he wouldn't do it again, and he hasn't, but he's careless and haphazard. Would you really trust Guy's life to somebody like that?"

"No, certainly not. I'll talk to Guy later."

"Thanks." She grimaced. "I guess I'm public enemy number one again," she said miserably.

"He'll understand when I explain it. All the same," he said with a glowering look, "he's not going to talk to you like that."

"Look at you bristle." She sighed, resting her chin on her hands. "A conceited woman would think you're head over heels in love with me."

He stared at her levelly. "I am head over heels in love with you," he said matter-of-factly.

Her breath stopped in her throat as she met the soft sensuality of his eyes and got lost in their green depths. "You what?" she faltered.

"I love you," he repeated. "Adore you. Worship the ground you walk on." He grinned. "We could go into the bedroom and I could tell you some more. But it's broad daylight and the radio's unplugged. And Mrs. Jenson won't confuse wailing with country music," he added, tongue-in-cheek.

She blushed, laughing. "Well, you do your share of that, too. It isn't all me!"

"I know," he said shamelessly. He sighed warmly and smiled at her. "I like just looking at you with your clothes off. Being able to make love to you is a bonus."

"I used to think I was oversized and plain before you came along," she murmured.

"Not anymore, I'll wager," he murmured, staring pointedly at her breasts. "If you're oversized, long live big girls."

She laughed. "Emmett!"

He grimaced. "I have to go to work. I don't want to," he added, when he got up and paused to kiss her on his way out. "But I don't get paid for kissing you."

"Pity," she whispered. "When you do it so well!"

He chuckled. "So do you."

"Emmett?"

He paused. "Hmm?"

"I love you, too," she said solemnly.

He smiled. "You tell me that with your body, every time we love each other." He traced a line down her straight nose. "I was telling you, the same way, but you didn't realize it, did you?"

She shook her head. Her eyes blazed with feeling. "I could walk on a cloud…"

"So could I." He bent and kissed her very softly. "One day, when the sharp edge wears off the hunger, maybe I'll be able to make love to you as tenderly as I want to in my heart," he whispered. "Right now, I can't tone down the desire I feel for you. If I have any regret, it's that."

"Have I complained?" she asked softly. "I want you just as badly, Emmett. It will keep." She smiled. She beamed. "I didn't know you loved me!"

"Well, you do, now." He pulled his hat low over his eyes. "Don't let it go to your head just because I walk into fence posts staring at you like a love-struck boy."

She put her hand over her heart, one of his

favorite postures, and grinned back at him. "Would I do that?"

His green eyes glittered with mischief. "We'd better find a rock station to listen to tonight," he murmured dryly.

She laughed with pure delight as he winked and went out the door. She had the world, she thought. She had the whole world. Emmett loved her! Everything was going to be perfect now.

The euphoria lasted until suppertime, when she went to feed Alistair. And she couldn't find him.

She looked through the house, in all his favorite places, but he wasn't anywhere to be seen. It was cold outside and threatening rain. Surely he wouldn't have gone out voluntarily! He hated the outdoors. He hated getting wet even more.

Then she remembered that Guy had been angry with her. The last time he'd been angry with her, he'd let Alistair out, and she almost hadn't got him back. But the boy wouldn't be that cruel again, would he?

She came back into the dining room, white in the face and obviously troubled.

"What's wrong?" Emmett asked, pausing

with a bowl of mashed potatoes in his hand and an uplifted spoon over his plate.

"Alistair's missing," she said unsteadily.

She didn't look at Guy, but everyone else did.

"I didn't let him out," Guy said. He felt frightened. He hadn't been near the big cat. He liked him, now. The last thing he'd ever want to do was hurt the animal. But everybody, including his father, was giving him looks like daggers. Everybody except Melody, who couldn't seem to look at him at all.

"I didn't!" Guy repeated. "I haven't even seen him today…!"

"You were mad because Melody didn't want you to go hunting with Bill," Emmett said curtly.

"I didn't let her cat out!" Guy got to his feet. "Dad, I'm not lying! I didn't do it! Why won't you believe me?"

"Because the last time you got mad at Melody, you turned him out into the streets of Houston," Emmett said icily. "And he wound up at the city pound, where instead of being put with new arrivals to be offered for adoption, he was accidentally mixed in a bunch scheduled for immediate termination!"

Melody's gasp was audible. Emmett had

never told her that. She shivered, and Guy saw it, and felt sick all over again. She looked devastated. He was sorry he'd been so angry about Bill.

He'd complained to one of the cowboys about being deprived of the hunting trip, and the cowboy had told him, tongue-in-cheek, that Bill couldn't get anybody to go with him after he'd accidentally wounded his last hunting partner. He'd added that Bill had damned near accidentally shot Melody herself a couple of weeks back, too. Guy hadn't known that. It had surprised and then pleased him that Melody had argued about letting him go. He wanted to ask her about it over supper and apologize. He'd been about to, when Melody couldn't find Alistair. And right now Guy felt in danger of becoming the entrée instead of a fellow diner.

Emmett put the mashed potatoes down. "Let's go," he said, tossing his napkin onto the table. "Everybody outside. We're going to find Alistair if it takes all night. Then," he added with a cold glare at his eldest son, "you and I are going to have a long talk about the future."

"You can't send me to military school." Guy choked. "I won't go!"

"You'll go," Emmett said, and kept walking. Melody barely heard him. She was too frightened for Alistair to notice much of what was being said. Guy had seemed so friendly, until she'd argued over that hunting trip. He was never going to accept her. He hated her. He had to, in order to put her pet at risk a second time. She was devastated.

So was Guy. He was going to be banished because of something he hadn't even done. He was going to be sent away. Military school. Demerits. Uniforms. No sister and brother to play with. No ranch.

"No," he said to himself. "No, I won't go!"

The others had gone out the door. Guy rushed to his room and got the few things he couldn't do without, including his allowance. He went back through the house, his heart pounding like mad, into his father's study. There was a small telephone journal, where important numbers were kept. His mother's number was there. He'd always wanted to use it, but he hadn't had the nerve. Now he did. He had absolutely nothing left to lose.

The phone rang and rang, and Guy watched the door nervously, chewing on his lip. He didn't want to be caught. He had to get away, but he needed a place to go. His mother was his only hope. She loved him. He knew she did, even if his father didn't.

"Hello?"

"Mom?" His voice wavered. "Mom, it's me. Guy."

"Guy!" There was excitement in her soft voice. "How are you? Does your father know you're calling me?" she added hesitantly.

"Mom, he's got a new wife," he began.

"Yes, I know. Randy's sister." She didn't even sound upset. "Melody is sweet and kind. She'll be good to you. I'm happy that your father has finally found someone he can really love, Guy…"

"But she hates me," he wailed. "She blames me for stuff I don't do. Look, can I come and live with you? They don't really want me here!"

There was a pause. "Son, you know I'd love nothing better. I really would love to have you. But, you see… I'm pregnant. And I'm having a hard time. I can't really look after you right now, having to stay in bed so much. But after the baby comes…" she added. "Guy? Guy?"

There was nothing but a dial tone on the other end of the line.

Guy stood looking at the replaced receiver. His mother was pregnant. She was going to have a baby. Not his father's baby. Randy's baby. That meant she was certainly never going to come back. She would have another family of her own, Randy's children.

Now, Guy thought numbly, he had no one at all. His father was remarried and would have other children, too. His mother didn't want him. He had nobody in the whole world.

He turned and walked out the front door. The rain was starting to come down in sheets. It was cold, and his jacket wasn't waterproof, but he really didn't care. He had nothing left to lose. His home, his secure life, his father, his mother, his family were all nothing but memories. He was unwanted and unloved.

Well, he thought with bitter sorrow, perhaps he could make it alone. He had twenty dollars in his pocket and he didn't mind hard work. There had to be someplace he could go where nobody would care about his age.

He started walking across the field toward the main highway. He didn't look back.

"Alistair!" Melody wailed. They'd been searching for half an hour, with no success at all. The big tabby cat hadn't turned up yet.

"You won't stop me this time," Emmett said angrily as they paused just inside the barn. "Guy won't be hurt by a little discipline. I'm going to enroll him in the same military school where I went when I was a boy."

"But he was getting used to me," Melody said miserably. "I know he was. I shouldn't have said anything about Bill…"

"And let him go off with the man and get killed?" He stared at her. "Melody, part of being a parent is knowing when to say no for a child's own good. You have to expect rebellion and tantrums, and not let yourself be swayed by them. Parenting is a rough job. Loving a child isn't enough. You have to prepare him to live in a hostile world."

"I guess there's more to it than I realized." She looked up at him. "Guy is so like you," she said gently. "I care about him. I don't want him to be hurt."

"Neither do I, but education isn't a punishment. I think he'll like it. I was homesick at first, but I loved it after the first two weeks. If he doesn't take to it," he added quietly, "he can come back home."

She smiled through her sadness. "You're a nice man."

"I'm a wet man," he replied. "Let's look for a few more minutes…"

"Emmett!" Amy shouted. "Emmett, he's here, he's here!"

"What?" He went into the barn, following her excited voice.

Emmett and Melody peered over into the corn crib and there, curled up on some hay, was a sleepy, purring Alistair.

"Oh, you monster!" Melody grumbled. She picked him up and cradled him close, murmuring softly to him.

"Found your cat, did you?" Larry, the eldest of the cowboys, asked with a smile. "Meant to tell you he'd got out, but we had a few head get lost and I had to go help hunt them. He ran out past me when I was talking to Ellie Jenson in the kitchen. Guess my spurs spooked him," he added ruefully. "No harm done, though, I suppose, was there? I'll be more careful next time, boss."

He tipped his hat and went to put up the tack he was carrying, water dripping off his hat.

Emmett and Melody exchanged horrified glances.

"Guy!" she whispered.

He drew in a deep breath. "Well, I guess I'll eat crow for a month," he muttered. "Come on. I might as well get it over with."

But it wasn't that easy. They went back into the house and the telephone was ringing off the hook. Mrs. Jenson had gone home an hour earlier, and Guy was apparently unwilling to pick up the receiver.

Emmett grabbed it up. "Hello?"

"Emmett! Thank God! It's Adell," she said.

Hearing her voice threw him off balance. He'd avoided talking to her for two years. Now, it was like hearing any woman's voice.

"Hello, Adell," he said pleasantly. "What can I do for you?"

"It's Guy," she said. "I've been trying to get you for a half hour. Guy called, and he sounded pretty desperate. He wanted to come and live with me, but I blurted out about the baby, and he hung up. I'm so worried. I didn't mean to tell him like that, Emmett. I didn't mean it to sound as if I didn't love him or want him…!"

"It's all a misunderstanding," Emmett said gently. "Now don't worry. He's hiding in his room and we'll get it straightened out. He'll be fine."

"I knew it would be hard for the kids when you got married again, but Melody's so sweet," she said softly. "She's just what the four of you need. The boys will worship her when they get used to her, and so will Amy."

"They already do," he said. "I've been pretty bullheaded over this, Adell. I'm sorry."

"I did it the wrong way," she confessed. "I

ran when I should have stood up and been honest with you. I guess if we'd really loved each other it would have been different. But I didn't know what love was until Randy came along." She hesitated. "I hope you know what I'm talking about."

"I do now," he said, staring quietly at Melody. "Oh, yes, I understand now."

"Let me know about Guy?"

"Of course. Adell, I'm glad for you and Randy, about the baby."

"We're ecstatic," she said. "I can hardly wait. A baby might be just the thing for the kids."

"You can bring it down to meet them when it's born," he said.

"Thanks. I will. But what I meant was if you and Melody had one of your own eventually, it would bring them closer to her."

He stared at Melody and flushed as the glory of fathering her child made his knees weak.

"Emmett?" Adell called.

"What? Oh. Yes. You can call the kids or write to them if you want," he said absently. "They can come and visit, too, when it's convenient. Or you and Randy can come down here. Tell him I won't hit him."

"He knows that. We both felt guilty over

what he'd done to you, for a long time. I'm glad it worked out."

"So am I. I'll have Guy call you back."

"That would be nice. Tell him I love him, and that I didn't mean he wasn't welcome here."

"I will." He hung up, his eyes slow and warm on Melody's face. "Adell thinks I should make you pregnant," he mused.

She caught her breath. "Well!"

He moved toward her, and paused to frame her face in his big, lean hands. "I think I should, too," he whispered. "Not right away, not until we're really a family. But I'd like it very much if we had a child together, Melody." He bent and drew his lips softly over hers.

"So would I." She clung to him, giving him back the kiss. She smiled warmly. "But for now, we'd better tell Guy that he isn't going to be banished to Siberia."

"Good point."

They went to his room and knocked. There was no answer. With a rueful smile, Emmett pushed it open, but Guy wasn't there.

Emmett looked around. Some of Guy's favorite possessions were missing, including that whittling knife that Melody had given him. He looked at her with fear in his eyes.

"He's run away, hasn't he?" she asked with faint panic.

His face was grim. "I'm afraid that's just what he's done," he replied.

Chapter 11

Jacobsville seemed to be a long way from anywhere, Guy thought, huddled miserably in his jacket while rain poured down on his bare head and soaked his sneakers. He was cold and getting colder by the minute. He should have taken time to search for the raincoat he could never find, but he'd been afraid someone would try to stop him.

After a few wet minutes, he managed to flag down a family of Mexicans driving toward Houston. With his meager Spanish, painstakingly taught to him by his bilingual father, he made them understand that he was on his way to his family. They smiled and nodded and gestured him into the crowded car of smiling, welcoming faces. People, he thought, were generally pretty nice. He was pleasantly surprised. Too bad he couldn't say that for his own family. They'd probably find Melody's cat dead and nobody would speak to him for the rest of his life. It wasn't his fault, but he guessed maybe he deserved it for what he'd done in Houston.

The Mexican family stopped at Victoria to get gas, and Guy had second thoughts about continuing on to Houston. He might as well try to find a place to stay here. Victoria was big enough that he could get lost in it.

He found a vacant lot where a small building stood with its door ajar. It was still raining. He darted into the shack and came face-to-face with a couple of men who looked as if murder might be their favorite Sunday pastime.

It took forever just to get the kids into Emmett's Bronco and strapped in. All the while, the rain was getting worse and Melody was chewing on her fingernails. They'd called the local police and a bolo went out over the air to law enforcement vehicles. Emmett had a CB unit and a scanner in the Bronco, and the scanner was turned on so that they'd hear immediately if Guy was spotted.

Emmett was actually able to track the boy down the highway at the end of the ranch road, until the footprints abruptly stopped.

He got back into the vehicle, his hat dripping water. "This is as far as he walked," he said tersely, turning toward Melody. "Thank God for thick mud and a light drizzling rain. I tracked him to the other side of the road. He's headed that way, toward Victoria."

He wheeled the vehicle around in the road and set off with grim determination toward the city.

"I hope to God whoever he was riding with needed gas, and that he found some decent person and not a pervert to get into the car with."

"He's a smart boy," Melody said gently, touching his arm. "He'll be all right, Emmett. I know he will." She grimaced. "Oh, it's my fault!"

"No, it's not," he said tersely. "It takes a little work to turn five people into a family. It doesn't happen overnight, you know."

"I'm learning that. All the same, Guy's more important to me than Alistair, even if I do love the stupid cat," she added quietly, staring worriedly through the misty windshield.

It took forever to get into the city. Then Emmett stopped at the nearest gas station before he proceeded to the next few. They were almost at the far end of town before an attendant remembered a bareheaded boy in a leather bomber jacket and jeans and sneakers.

"He was pretty wet," the man said with a grin. "Came in with a family of Mexicans, but he didn't want to go on to Houston with them. I had to explain. Kid spoke really lousy Spanish," he murmured sheepishly.

"Did you see which way he went?"

"No. I'm sorry, but we got busy and I didn't notice. Can't have gotten far, though. It's only been ten or fifteen minutes, and he didn't hitch another ride, I'm sure of that."

"Thanks. Thanks a lot. Okay if I leave the Bronco here while we look for him?"

"Sure, it's okay! Just park it anywhere. I'll look out for it."

"Much obliged."

Emmett pulled it out of the way and parked it. He turned to the others. "We're going to spread out and go over this area of town like tar paper. Amy, you go with Melody. Polk, with me. If you find him, sing out."

"All right, Emmett," Amy said politely. "We'll find him."

"God, I hope so," he said heavily. It was already dark. The streetlights were a blessing, but any city was dangerous at night. They had to find the boy soon, or they might never find him.

They piled out of the Bronco and Emmett paused to look hard at Melody. "Don't go anywhere you don't feel comfortable. I don't like having any of us out on these streets at night. Stay where it's lighted. If you get in trouble, scream. I'll hear you."

She smiled up at him. "Amy and I both will," she mused.

"I can scream good, Emmett," Amy said. "Want to hear me?"

"Not just yet, thanks," he murmured, tugging a pigtail. "Get going."

Melody and Amy went down one street, Emmett another. They met a policeman cruising by, and Emmett stopped to talk to him. He explained the situation.

"We got the bolo on the radio," the patrolman, an elderly man, replied. "We're watching for him. He's pretty safe if he's still in this area. Hope you find him."

"So do I," Emmett said quietly. "He's got the wrong end of the stick. He thinks we don't care about him because we have to say no sometimes."

"Prisons are full of kids who never got said no to," the policeman mused. "Might tell him that."

"He'll get an earful, after he gets hugged half to death," Emmett said with a wry smile.

"That's how I raised my four. One's a lawyer now." With a twinkle in his eyes he added, "Of course, the others are respectable..."

Emmett laughed despite his fears and lifted his hand as the patrol car pulled away into the darkness.

Down the street, Melody was huddled in her coat, drawing Amy closer as the rain began to fall again. She looked and looked, and found nothing. Finally, yielding to defeat, she turned and guided Amy back toward the service station.

The shack in the empty lot had caught her eye earlier, but she hadn't paid it much mind because she was sure Guy would be trying to make some distance.

Now, she wasn't so certain.

"Let's take a look in there, just in case," she told Amy. "Stay close."

"Okay, Melody."

They moved quickly toward the shack, and as they approached it, loud voices could be heard. There was a violent thumping noise, and the ramshackle door suddenly moved and Guy came tearing out of it. His face was bleeding and his jacket was half off. A thin, dirty man was holding the half that was off, dragging at it.

"I said, I want the damned jacket!" the surly voice repeated.

"It's Guy!" Amy exclaimed.

"Yes." Melody's eyes blazed with anger. She was never so happy for her size. "Stay behind me," she called as she broke into a run.

Guy was fighting the man, but the other one had a stick and was raising it.

"You leave my son alone!" Melody yelled at them.

The men stopped suddenly and gaped at her. So did a shocked, delighted Guy. While they were gaping, she sailed right into the one who had Guy by the sleeve, performed a jump kick accompanied by a cry that would have made her instructor applaud and landed her foot squarely into the attacker's gut.

Guy barely had time for one astonished look at her threatening stance. Loosened by the man's collapse, Guy turned quickly to place a hard kick in the other man's groin before he could bring down the stick he was holding up and then planted a hard fist right into his

cheek. The second man went down with a little
cry of pain and landed unconscious.

"Are you all right?" Melody asked Guy,
dragging him close to hug him. "Oh, you
holy terror, if you ever do anything like this
again…!" She was barely coherent, crying
and mumbling, searching his face for cuts and
bruises, brushing back his unruly damp hair.
But the whole time she was holding him as his
mother once had when he stumbled and fell,
when he was hurt or afraid.

Big boys weren't supposed to like this sort of
thing, of course, much less tolerate it. And he
was going to twist away from her any minute
now and make some curt remark. But just for
a minute or so, it wouldn't hurt to be hugged
and cried over.

"How did you do that?" he asked, aghast.

"Oh, that. Well, I have a belt in tae kwon do.
Just a brown. I never finished my training."

"Just a brown!" He caught his breath. "That
was great! Like watching Chuck Norris or
Jean-Claude Van Damme," he added, nam-
ing his two idols. "Listen, could you teach me
some of that?"

"You and the other kids, too," she promised.
"Then next time, you'll be prepared." She grimaced as she studied him. "Listen, Alistair's

fine, one of the men accidentally let him out," she said miserably, drawing back. "I'm so sorry. All of us are sorry for blaming you. For heaven's sake, you're more important than a cat, even if he was the only friend I had! Your father was frantic, and so were the rest of us!"

Guy felt strange. He sort of smiled and couldn't stop. "I'm all right." He looked down at the squirming, groaning men. "Uh, it might not be a bad idea if we leave," he suggested, taking her arm. "You and I were pretty much a match for them, but we've Amy to think about."

"You're right. I do wish I had a gun," she muttered, glaring at them.

"Can you shoot one?" Guy asked on the way down the street.

"Sure I can shoot," she said. "I've won awards."

"Really?"

"You still can't go hunting with Bill," she said curtly, glaring at him. "He'd kill you. He's not responsible with a gun. If you go hunting, I'll take you, or your father will. Or we'll all go. But I'm not shooting anything, even if I do go along, and I couldn't skin a squirrel if my life depended on it."

"We wouldn't go hunting to kill stuff," Guy

said. "We'd go hunting so that we can grumble about how cold it was and how much big game got away. And so that we can sit and talk away from cars and horns and clocks."

"Oh."

He shrugged. "It would be all right if you came along, I guess. We could shoot at targets."

"I can shoot, too," Amy said. "I have a bow and arrow that Emmett made me."

"Polk can bring his atl-atl," Guy remarked. "We'd be the most dangerous family in the woods."

Melody laughed. She felt exhausted now. They came to the street where the service station sat on the corner, and there were Emmett and Polk coming toward them.

"Guy!" Emmett shouted.

The boy ran to him, and Emmett lifted him off the ground in a bear hug. "My God, you are something! I wish I'd hit you harder when you were a little kid!"

"I guess you should have, all right," Guy murmured, fighting tears. "I'm sorry, Dad...!"

"I'm sorry," Emmett corrected grimly. He put the boy down. "We're all sorry. If you had any idea how worried we were!" His green eyes began to glitter. "Son, if you ever, ever do anything like this to us again, I'll... I'll...!"

"He's trying to think up something bad enough to threaten you with," Melody translated, grinning at him. "It may take a while."

"Some men were beating up Guy, Emmett," Amy said excitedly. "Melody knocked one of them out, and Guy hit the other one. They're lying in the dirt back there."

"You'd better show me those men," Emmett said. The remark Amy had made about Melody went right over his head. He was incensed that anyone should hit his child. "Why were they beating on you?" Emmett asked slowly.

"They wanted my jacket," Guy said, grimacing. "I should have had better sense than to go in there in the first place, but I was wet and miserable and I didn't think. They were tramps, I think—maybe hitchhikers."

"Let's check this out, just in case," Emmett said, and he looked pretty dangerous, Guy thought as they walked together toward the shack. But a police car came by before they reached it. Emmett told the officer what had happened, and he was told that there had been some trouble with transients lately. He went to check, but the men were long gone. Which was just as well.

The fighting Deverells climbed back into their Bronco and went home.

* * *

A little later, with three exhausted kids tucked up in bed before they managed to re-hash the exciting incident, Melody lay curled up in Emmett's hard arms, smiling with pure bliss after the most tender loving she'd ever known.

"This is what I wanted it to be on our wedding night," he said drowsily. "But I was too desperate for you." He bent and brushed his mouth lovingly over her soft lips, smiling warmly.

"When we get around to making a baby, I want it to be like it was tonight," she whispered into his warm throat. "We've never been closer than this."

"I know." He cradled her body to his and stretched lazily. "Guy's going to be Alistair's champion from now on, I imagine," he murmured.

"Friends to the end. Alistair's sleeping with him."

"He's your champion, too. You should have heard him telling Polk what you did to that tramp on his behalf." He glanced at her. "Polk told him what you said, about his being more important to you than Alistair. He's been strutting all night."

"He's a very special boy. But he's much more sensitive than he looks." She traced his thick eyebrows. "We'll have to remember that. Both of us. And no military school. If he goes, I'm going with him."

"For protection?"

"Laugh if you like, but I'm a brown belt in tae kwon do."

"What?"

She shrugged, smiling at his surprise. "Didn't you wonder how I was able to drop a man that size so easily? I didn't have anything else to do on long winter nights, so I enrolled in a Korean karate class. It was very educational."

"No wonder you didn't balk when I asked you to go with Amy to look for Guy. I worried about doing that. Men are going to feel protective about their women. It's their nature."

"I know that. I don't mind. Just as long as you know that I'm not helpless all the time." She rolled over and kissed his chest, feeling his breath catch as her lips pressed through the thick hair to the hard, warm flesh beneath it. "Of course," she whispered, "there are times when I really enjoy being helpless."

"Is this one of them?" he murmured, coaxing her mouth closer.

"I think so."

"Good. Let's be helpless together…"

He rolled her over and very quickly, the friendly banter turned to something much more serious and intense.

Randy and a very pregnant Adell came to visit two months later. The children accepted her condition without comment, and there were no problems.

By the time Emmett and his family drove Adell and Randy back to the airport, they were friends. Randy, who looked so much like his sister, was obviously the end of Adell's rainbow.

"Nice to see them so happy," Emmett remarked as he and Melody watched the other couple walk off toward the loading ramp, arms close around each other.

"Yes, isn't it?" Melody asked with a sigh. "Emmett, I'm so happy I could burst."

"So am I." He bent to kiss her, very softly. "And the kids were so good, weren't they? I could hardly believe they were the same bunch that put on their Thanksgiving Indian costumes and attacked that car of Florida tourists that got lost on the place last week. We really are going to have to start enforcing some new codes of behavior."

"Oh, maybe not," Melody said. "They've been so good today…"

"Excuse me?"

A uniformed security guard with a grim expression tapped on Emmett's shoulder.

"Yes?" Emmett asked politely.

"Someone said those might be your kids…?"

He gestured toward the concourse. Emmett noticed three things. An empty pet carrier. A screaming, running woman. Three laughing children holding equal parts of an enormous, friendly python. It looked almost identical to a Far Side cartoon by Gary Larson that the twins had just been looking at in the book he'd bought them earlier…

Emmett didn't dare do what he felt like doing. Hysterical laughter was not going to help him. He looked at the security guard. He put his hand over his heart. "Officer," he said pleasantly, "I have never seen those kids before in my life…"

Melody gave him a glare that was good for two headaches and a lonely night, and went running down the concourse after the children.

* * * * *